To Karen,
Do you think Mr. McFarland
would approve?
Best wishes
Sheena

A Sheltered Life

A Sheltered Life

SHEENA PENNIE

Order this book online at www.trafford.com
or email orders@trafford.com
Most Trafford titles are also available at major online book retailers.

Printed in the United States of America.

ISBN: 978-1-4269-6735-1 (sc)
ISBN: 978-1-4269-6736-8 (hc)
ISBN: 978-1-4269-6737-5 (e)

Library of Congress Control Number: 2011907585

Trafford rev. 06/02/2011

 www.trafford.com

North America & International
toll-free: 1 888 232 4444 (USA & Canada)
phone: 250 383 6864 ♦ fax: 812 355 4082

Dedication

A Sheltered Life is dedicated to my parents, Barbara and Archie Pennie and to my brother Ross. This story was inspired by my adopted sister, Patsy, who lived with us for twelve years.

Acknowledgements

I would be remiss if I didn't acknowledge the 'gentle' reminders to finish this story by my dear friend Louise and the glowing support from her teenage daughter Sophie. The easy-to-understand explanations of DNA matches and the bone marrow transplant procedure are courtesy of my brother, Ross, an infectious diseases specialist. My husband, Tim, who laughed and cried at all the right moments, is to be commended for 'living' this story with me. Of course, there would have been no story had my son not been mugged on the bus by a gang of street kids. You see, Alex, things do happen for a reason.

A Sheltered Life

Chapter One

Ping!, rattle, bang, thump, 'Mum!' Just like clockwork every afternoon, Fiona heard the Twiss long-case grandfather clock strike 5:30, the key in the side door turn, the door slam shut, the backpack drop to the floor, followed by the unmistakable greeting from her 15-year-old son, Connor. Today's version of 'Mum!', though, sounded decidedly more anxious than usual.

"Anything wrong, Connor?" called Fiona from the kitchen. "You sound upset about something, honey. Come and tell me what's happened."

Connor stormed into the kitchen, his face like thunder, and ranted, "I told you I didn't like taking the bus home when it gets dark so early. It's all your fault! You made me go to that stupid school and now because of it I got mugged on the bus by a bunch of street kids. They saw my stupid school uniform, swarmed me and stole my Walkman."

"Oh, Connor, that's awful. Did they hurt you, sweetheart?" said Fiona, approaching her son with open arms.

Shaking his head, Connor backed away, "They kept shoving me, saying I was just a rich kid whose parents buy him everything he wants. After they grabbed my Walkman, they got off the bus at the next stop. I went and told the bus driver what had happened and he just rolled his eyes and shrugged his shoulders. I was really scared, Mum. I hate those kids!"

"They had no right to do that to you, Connor. Unfortunately, they feel threatened by kids like you and this is the only way they know how to cope. Stealing from you, and scaring you in the process, makes them feel superior. You did the right thing, though, giving up your Walkman. Picking a fight with them would have made the whole situation much worse."

Connor dropped his head and stepped toward his mother who responded with a warm hug. "It's OK," Fiona said reassuringly, "I'll call Ottawa Transpo in the morning to report it and find out why the bus driver didn't offer to help. Tomorrow, though, why not carry your uniform in your gym bag and change once you get to school?" She would also call Worcester Academy and speak with Headmaster MacFarlane to see if other students had been subjected to the same harassment.

Connor was right about it being his parents' decision, not his, to attend Worcester Academy, a private school located in a very tony part of Ottawa, Canada's capital. And it was also true that he was an easy target for snide remarks and name-calling as he traveled on the bus to and from Worcester wearing his telltale crested blazer and grey trousers.

Things certainly had changed since Fiona attended high school in Ottawa. At that time, Fiona never witnessed any violence, gangs, intolerance or drug use. She wasn't sure if it was her strict upbringing that had sheltered her from 'unsavoury characters and shady goings-on', as her father put it, or whether her lack of awareness and knowledge of all things unsavoury stemmed from the fact that she had been a member of the gifted program or "suck class" as it was called by most of the student body.

Although it had been a difficult decision to change Connor's school and to separate him from his friends at St. Stephen's, Fiona knew that removing him from what was escalating into an extremely unsafe and academically challenged environment was the right thing to do. After all, it had been 25 years since she graduated from high school; kids were now being exposed to all sorts of temptations and boundary extensions that she could never have imagined.

In addition to Connor's mugging, conversation around the dinner table that evening included Fiona's 14-year-old 'bonus' (she disliked the word 'step') daughter Frances' recent rugby victory and her husband Michael's interview on CNN.

"Your Mum tells me you had a rather rough time on the bus this afternoon, Connor," said Michael as he served him a second helping of Maltese potatoes and ricotta pie, "I'm sorry you were the brunt of the anger and frustration felt by those kids. It's hard for us to put ourselves in their shoes."

"Yeah, shoes they probably stole from someone. You should have heard the awful things they said about me," said Connor glumly. "Oh yeah, as if my day couldn't get any worse, I got this in social studies class today." Connor rifled through his pockets and thrust a crumpled letter at his mother. In it, Fiona read that all students in Grade 11, Connor's year, were required to complete forty hours of volunteer work before the end of June. Since the school year had just begun, that meant Connor would have nine months to complete his forty hours. There was a line at the bottom of the letter for parents to sign indicating they understood that non completion of the volunteer service would result in a failed year.

"It's not fair!" Connor wailed. "Forty hours is way too long. What good will it do me to volunteer at some stupid place? It's not as if I'll learn anything. I have way more important things to do like racing with the ski team, learning to drive the Jetta and playing hockey. Anyway, I don't have anywhere to volunteer and now I don't have a Walkman."

"It's not just Worcester students who have to volunteer. All Grade 11's in the Province of Ontario are in the same boat as you are," said Fiona brightly. "Let's go online after dinner and see what types of organizations are looking for volunteers. We could even look for a new Walkman."

"I'm going to volunteer at a physiotherapy clinic, when it's my turn next year," interjected Frances.

"Well, goodie for you, Frances. This isn't about you, if you hadn't noticed," snapped Connor.

"Wait a minute, Connor," said Fiona. "Frances has a point. She's interested in physiotherapy so naturally she would want to volunteer where she would learn more about it."

"Sorry, Frances," said Connor, "I'm still bummed about those street kids stealing my Walkman. Can I get the new one with the noise-reduction headphones?"

"I think that's worth considering, but in the meantime let's concentrate on finding you somewhere to volunteer," reassured Fiona.

Fiona Hamilton had been married to Michael Kellaher for ten years. Connor was five and Frances four when they became a 'blended' family and it still amazed her how much the two siblings resembled each other. When they entered Worcester Academy together (Connor in Grade 10 and Frances in Grade 9), they were often asked if they were twins.

At first, they disavowed any knowledge of each other, as if admitting they were related would somehow ruin their chance of completing high school blissfully and worry free. However, as they became more accustomed to their new surroundings and more relaxed about being at the same school (even sharing the same friends), they actually took to referring to themselves as brother and sister. They blithely adopted an 'if you can't beat 'em join 'em' attitude which made Fiona marvel at her children's ability to adapt and make the most of any situation they found themselves in.

Fiona and Michael owned a public relations firm – Hamilton & Kellaher – one of the largest in the country. As President, Fiona oversaw the administration of the firm and was in the enviable position of being able to set her own office hours so that she could be home in time for Connor's and Frances' arrival from school. She'd heard too many horror stories about teenagers being home alone between the hours of 4:00 pm and 6:00 pm and getting into all kinds of trouble.

After dinner and once he and his sister had finished the dishes, Connor sat at the kitchen table with the computer trying to find an organization that would benefit from the assistance of an unmotivated, hard-done-by and disinterested 15-year-old!

He finally settled on a homeless shelter not far from Worcester Academy. Once the proper introductions and paperwork were completed later that week, it was agreed that Connor would walk to the shelter after school three times a week and work at the front desk over the dinner hour answering the phone and taking messages.

For Connor, this was perfect. He wouldn't actually have to interact with the homeless people much, since they'd all be eating their dinner and the best part was he'd have access to a phone which meant he could organize his social calendar without any interruptions. The forty hours would be over in no time with little or no effort on his part and getting his new Walkman would be icing on the cake.

Fiona, on the other hand, hoped that the experience would, in fact, provide him with some insight into the lives of those less fortunate. Only time would tell.

Chapter Two

On his first day of volunteering, Connor walked to the homeless shelter after school. A former residence for the Catholic Church's Sisters of Charity, it still bore all the trappings of a building constructed for religious purposes. As he entered the front door, he was greeted by a large statue of the Madonna in the centre of the foyer. She gazed down at him serenely, her hands outstretched, palms up. It gave him the creeps and he walked by her as quickly as he could. To his left, he could hear the noise of tables being set for dinner and could just make out the smell of gravy and what he thought might be roast chicken.

He had no intention of venturing into the dining hall in case he encountered an actual homeless person. That would be even creepier than walking by the statue in the front hall. He'd been told to find Mrs. Bradley, the shelter's director, who would give him an idea of what he was expected to do. Luckily he saw her name on a door to his right and just as he was walking toward it a woman opened the door and came into the hall. She was about his mother's age and smiled as she approached Connor.

"You must be Connor Munro," she said shaking his hand. "We're so pleased that you volunteered to help out here."

"Thank you Mrs. Bradley," replied Connor, "although, I'm not sure I can be much help."

"Of course, you can. Just come with me to our reception desk and I'll introduce you to our telephone system. We'd like you to answer the phone over the dinner hour, take messages and then hand them to me before you leave. If the call is urgent, please come and find me right away. I'll be in the kitchen plating dinners for our clients."

They walked back to the centre of the foyer, past the Madonna (at least they walked behind her so that Connor didn't get the feeling her eyes were following him), to a long desk just to the left of the entrance to the dining hall. At one end of the desk was a stack of wire trays with a label on each one: Mail In; Mail Out; Courier In; Courier Out. At the other end was a large contraption with buttons and flashing lights attached to a headset.

"Well, here's your desk, Connor," said Mrs. Bradley. "Don't worry about those trays. You won't be receiving any mail or courier packages at this time of the day. Here is the headset that you will wear. It makes it easier to answer the phone." She fitted the headset over the top of Connor's head, rested the earpiece over his right ear and adjusted the microphone just under his chin. "How does that feel?"

"Not bad," said Connor surprisingly, "I feel like those mission control guys you see on TV. What do all these buttons do?"

"During the day, those buttons connect to the staff here in the building. But after hours, the only one you need to press is 'Line One' when you hear the phone ringing", said Mrs. Bradley pointing to the large green button at the top of the telephone console. "Once you press it, you will say into the microphone, 'Rideau Terrace Shelter, Connor speaking'. Most of the callers will ask for information like our address and our hours of operation. Other calls will be for me, at which time you may take a message or ask if they mind holding while you come and find me. Have you any questions?"

"It seems pretty straight forward. Where will you be if I need to find you?"

"Just through those doors to the left," replied Mrs. Bradley pointing to the dining hall.

As Mrs. Bradley headed toward the noise and smells of the meals that were being prepared for the homeless people, Connor sat down behind the desk and put his backpack underneath. She hadn't explained to him how to make outgoing calls, but Connor was sure it would be pretty easy and since no one was watching him every minute, he could use the time to call Kit and Steph and set up their weekly street hockey game.

Connor's first shift was a piece of cake; only a couple of calls, nothing out of the ordinary. At this rate, thought Connor thankfully, he would complete his 40 hours of volunteer service before Christmas and never have to actually see or speak to a homeless person.

His second shift changed his life forever.

Things started out smoothly. Connor could hear cutlery clanking on plates and chairs scraping the floor. Not many voices, though; either the 'clients', as Mrs. Bradley called them, were too busy eating or they had nothing to say to each other. Then, all of a sudden he heard shouting – a cacophony of raised voices all at once.

A man wearing a red woollen hat pulled down past his eyebrows ran through the dining hall doors straight to Connor frantically shouting at him to call 9-1-1.

"What's happened?" asked Connor as he punched the numbers, picturing a deadly knife fight over a chocolate pudding.

"Switcher has collapsed and hit his head! He's bleeding to death. Hurry up man! Get the ambulance. Quick!" screamed the man, waving his arms inches from Connor's face.

Connor froze when the 9-1-1 operator asked him what his emergency was and whether he needed fire, police or ambulance. He couldn't remember why he was calling or where he was calling from. The foyer was now filled with people and there was so much noise he had to plug his left ear in order to hear the operator repeat the question.

"Um, I'm not sure. No, wait, someone has fallen and hit their head; there's a lot of blood. Ambulance, that's what we need. No, I don't know who it is. No, I don't know if it's a man or a woman. I just answer the phone here. Oh, God, what's the address? It's called the Rideau Terrace Shelter. You're sending the ambulance? My name? It's, um, Connor, Connor Munro. Is the ambulance on its way? Thanks." Connor hung up the phone as Mrs. Bradley approached him, her face full of concern.

"Is the ambulance on its way, Connor?" she asked, patting him on the shoulder.

"Yes, it should be here in a couple of minutes. What happened in there? Was there a fight? I heard all this shouting."

"No, no fight. One of our young men fainted and hit his head rather badly. Are you all right? Quite a lot of commotion on your second night with us, eh?"

"I'm fine now but I sure was nervous there for a moment. My mind went blank when I called 9-1-1. The operator must think I'm an idiot."

"Not at all Connor. You handled the situation brilliantly," said Mrs. Bradley reassuringly. "I'm going back to lend a hand in the dining hall. Please show the paramedics where to go when they arrive."

Connor heard the screeching siren and saw the flashing lights as the ambulance drew up to the front doors. In seconds, two paramedics were wheeling a gurney toward him. Without being asked, Connor directed them to the dining hall where he saw a dozen or so people crowding around the man who had fainted. The paramedics moved in swiftly to assess the young man's injuries. The crowd moved back to give them room. Connor watched as they tended to the wound on his forehead. How could they tell how bad it was with all that blood on his face? The young man lay silent and motionless. Was he dead, thought Connor?

Cases containing medical equipment and supplies were clicked open and speedy hands delved into their contents. Connor was relieved to see that in no time at all bandages were applied, intravenous drips were inserted and the young man was lifted gently onto the waiting gurney.

As the paramedics wheeled the young man past him, Connor could see that underneath all the gauze and bandages, the young man was, in fact, just a kid – about the same age as Connor.

When Fiona swung into the shelter's circular drive, Connor was not pacing outside like last time waiting for her. Rather, she could see him through the glass doors speaking with a woman who looked about her own age. They appeared deep in conversation and she had to honk twice to get his attention.

He ran to the car and started speaking rapidly and incoherently even before he'd opened the car door. All she managed to grasp was "kid – blood – 9-1-1 – ambulance".

"Slow down, Connor," said Fiona, as she rolled down his window, "I can't understand a word you're saying."

"He's just a kid, Mum, about my age," said Connor as he got into the car, "I had to call 9-1-1."

"Start at the beginning," replied Fiona, slowly pulling out of the driveway.

"I was talking to Kit on the phone when this crazy guy ran out of the dining hall over to the reception desk and screamed at me that somebody called 'Switcher' had collapsed and was bleeding to death. He shouted at me to call 9-1-1, but I just froze."

"It's OK Connor. That's a normal reaction. I assume you did make the call, though."

"Yeah, I did but I couldn't remember the name of the shelter or the address. I felt like such an idiot until the operator told me that the address had come up on her screen. It didn't take long for the ambulance to come and then I saw all the blood on his face and a huge gash over his left eye. He's just a kid, Mum. I couldn't even tell if he was alive! What's he doing at a homeless shelter?"

As they drove home, Connor continued to describe the boy, his blood, his torn shirt, the blood, his ill-fitting cargo pants bulging with what Connor assumed were the boy's worldly possessions and the blood.

"Where will the ambulance take him?" asked Connor.

"If he's your age, they'll take him to the Children's Hospital just down the street from us. He'll be okay, Connor," assured Fiona as she reached over to squeeze Connor's hand. "He's lucky you were there to call the ambulance so quickly."

Chapter Three

The next morning at breakfast, Fiona watched as Connor ate his cereal in silence. Unlike Frances, who never said a word to anyone until she'd been up for a least an hour, Connor was a morning person, full of energy, chatter and noise. Today, though, something was different.

"You're awfully quiet, this morning, Connor," said Fiona.

"I didn't get much sleep. I couldn't stop thinking about that kid. Do you think he's alright?"

"I'm sure he's being well looked after at the hospital. If you're worried about him, you could always walk over to see him after dinner."

"I don't even know his real name. They called him Switcher at the shelter."

Fiona was surprised at her son's obvious concern for the boy from the shelter. A typical teenager, Connor's main interests focused on himself, his friends and his ever-growing collection of teenage-boy toys (computers, video games, skis/ skates, boom box and music). The fact that he was thinking about someone else's wellbeing seemed out of character for her son.

"I guess I could ask about him at the shelter when I go after school today," suggested Connor, as he stuffed his lunch into his backpack. "Frances, hurry up, we'll be late for the bus. I'm not waiting for you again. We almost missed it yesterday."

As Fiona watched the two of them head out the door, she wondered whether she should make some initial inquiries at the shelter or at the Children's Hospital. Then she stopped herself. She had to learn to let her children, particularly Connor, do things on their own. In this case, she would let him take the lead.

Fiona picked up Connor at the shelter, after his shift, and as he got into the car, she could see by the expression on his face that he had news to tell.

"He's still in hospital," reported Connor. "I heard some of the others talking about what happened. They say he fainted because he's very sick. No one seems to know why. So, I asked Mrs. Bradley, and she told me that he has leukemia. She also told me his name is Jesse Brown but she doesn't know why his street name is Switcher."

They drove in silence for a few minutes and then Connor asked his mother what leukemia was and whether Jesse would die. Fiona explained that she didn't know a great deal about the disease but she did say that many types of leukemia were now treatable and that some were even curable.

"Do you think I should go to the hospital to see him?" Connor asked.

"I think that would be very nice, Connor."

Again, Fiona was struck by her son's interest in the plight of someone less fortunate. She wondered whether all those stories she'd told him about her having to do volunteer work over the summer holidays when she was young had finally sunk in. Not that she'd had the choice. It was mandatory, scheduled and enforced by her mother Ann Hamilton – the volunteer Queen and community organizer! From the age of nine to nineteen, Fiona had stuffed envelopes, supervised mentally handicapped children, taught swimming at the 'Y', served meals (including Christmas dinners) to the elderly, prepared food hampers and driven for the Hospice, the Children's Aid Society and Meals on Wheels.

"Could you let me off at the hospital now, please?" asked Connor.

"Good idea!" replied Fiona.

She let him off at the main door and watched him enter the hospital and proceed to the information desk.

Chapter Four

Connor arrived home just before dinner, exited to tell everyone what had happened at the hospital. At the information desk, he'd asked for Jesse Brown and was told to go to the 6th floor, room 6046, bed 4.

As soon as the elevator opened on the 6th floor, there was such a foul smell that it made Connor feel sick to his stomach. So much so that he almost didn't get out. Determined to keep going, he plugged his nose and headed down the corridor looking for Switcher's room. Luckily it was at the far end of the hall where the smell had a chance to dissipate.

By the time Connor reached 6046, his nausea had subsided. In the large, square room, there were four beds; two on each side, separated by sets of white drapes hanging from curved tracks in the ceiling. Three of the sets of curtains were partially closed and faint murmurings could be heard emanating from behind them. But those surrounding bed No. 4 were open. Connor nervously approached the bed where he saw a boy lying with his eyes closed. His head above his left eye was heavily bandaged. His arms were pierced with needles attached to tubes hanging from a myriad of clear plastic bags that dangled from metal poles. Connor wasn't completely convinced that this was the same boy he'd seen at the shelter since that boy's face had been obscured by a bloody towel.

Connor cleared his throat and started to speak with his usual, "Um…, my name is Connor Munro. I volunteer at the shelter where you fell and hit your head. I was the one who called 9-1-1. I came by just to see if you were OK and if there was anything that I could bring you."

As Connor spoke, Jesse Brown's eyes remained closed but his head bobbed slightly leading Connor to notice the earphones in Jesse's ears. Connor's eyes followed the cord and saw that it was connected to a Walkman on the bedside table. There was a Nirvana sticker on the front of the Walkman that struck Connor as very familiar. Nirvana was his favourite band and Kurt Cobain was his current hero. He moved closer and saw that 'CM' had been scratched into the Walkman's bottom left-hand corner – Connor Munro. It was Connor's Walkman – stolen from him on the bus by that gang of street kids!

Connor drew his breath in sharply causing Jesse to open his eyes. Startled at seeing a stranger standing at the end of his bed, Jesse quickly removed the earphones, looked Connor up and down disdainfully and growled, "Who the hell are you?"

Realizing that Jesse had not heard a word he'd said, since the music from the Walkman was so loud, Connor explained again his reason for being there. As he spoke he couldn't help shifting his eyes back and forth from Jesse's face to the Walkman.

Once Connor had finished, there was a slight pause and then Jesse smiled slightly, raised his hand and gave him a weak but significant high-five.

"Thanks, man," said Jesse. "Sometimes I just black out and I wake up somewhere else. This is the first time I've ended up here, though. My head hurts like hell but they sure give you great painkillers!"

Connor pulled up the plastic guest chair and the two talked about music, hockey and cars; not about the Walkman or why Jesse lived on the street or what was in all the plastic bags dripping into Jesse's veins.

One thing Connor did ask was where Jesse got his street name.

"Why do they call you 'Switcher'?"

"It's 'cuz I'm right-handed but I switch to shoot left when I play hockey — freaks everyone out. Although it's been quite a while since I've been on the ice."

The explanation struck a chord with Connor since he also shot left although he was right-handed. From the intercom on the wall, a motherly voice announced that visiting hours were over. As Connor prepared to leave, he told Jesse he'd be back the next day with some *Car and Driver* magazines. Jesse nodded enthusiastically and they both instinctively flashed the peace sign at each other, saying "Peace out homie!" in unison. Connor left the hospital with a smile on his face and a warmth in his chest that he'd never felt before.

When he'd finished telling his family about his visit with Jesse, Fiona asked, "Why didn't you say anything about the Walkman?"

"After seeing him bandaged up with all those tubes sticking out of his arms, it just didn't seem all that important."

Chapter Five

The next day after school, Connor went straight home and picked out five of his favourite issues of *Car and Driver* magazine.

"I'm going to visit Jesse at the hospital, Mum," called Connor as he started out the door.

"Dinner's at 6:30. Tell Jesse we'd be pleased to get him anything he needs."

"Thanks, Mum," said Connor shutting the door behind him. Of all the other mothers he knew, his mother was the best. It didn't matter how many friends he brought home, usually at dinnertime, she would greet them warmly and just put out more plates, cutlery and food. She treated them like each one was her favourite, asking them about their home-life, school-life and love-life. She always remembered details from their answers to follow up on the next time she saw them. Many of his friends had even taken to calling her "Mom." Connor took great comfort in knowing that whatever happened in his life – good or bad – she would support him, encourage him and love him unconditionally.

Arriving at the door to Jesse's room, Connor could see that Jesse was sitting up and looking much brighter than the day before.

"Hi Connor," called Jesse. "I wasn't sure if you would visit me today."

Connor noticed that his Walkman was nowhere in sight. "I brought you some magazines I thought you might like to look at and some batteries for your Walkman."

He handed them to Jesse. "Thanks, man. I love cars. I don't know when I'll get my license, though. When do you get yours?"

"My birthday is in March but I start my driver's ED classes in February. My Mum says she'll take me to write my exam on my birthday. I can't wait to drive our Jetta."

Jesse nodded and put the magazines and batteries aside.

Connor pulled up the chair and asked Jesse about his illness. He learned that Jesse had something called acute leukemia - cancer of the blood. Jesse was quite matter-of-fact when he told Connor that he was, in fact, dying.

"Dying," exclaimed Connor. "You can't be dying! You have all these tubes and bags filled with medicine and doctors and nurses here to help you get better".

Jesse smiled slightly and explained to Connor that he had been diagnosed four years ago and had undergone extensive chemotherapy - twice. Both times, the leukemia had come back. And now, according to the doctors, Jesse's only hope was a bone marrow transplant.

Jesse then told Connor that he'd been living on the street since his mother's death from breast cancer a year ago. "She was only 41," said Jesse. "It was awful to see her fade away to skin and bone at the end and yet all she did was worry about me. I'm sure that if I hadn't been so sick, she would have taken better care of herself and she might be alive today."

"Where's your Dad?"

"I don't know who my Dad is. My mother never told me. I'm not even sure she knew. I do know that I was born in Ottawa but we moved to Toronto when I was two."

Jesse's life in Toronto had not been an easy one. His mother had difficulty finding both work and someone to take care of her young son. They moved constantly and Jesse had changed schools so many times he'd lost count. It was soon after his mother married a much older man that Jesse began to suffer physical abuse. Fuelled by alcohol and rage, Jesse's stepfather blamed him for everything that had gone wrong in his life – including his mother's death - and beat him as a consequence. Following his mother's funeral and what Jesse vowed would be his last beating, he packed his meagre belongings and headed back to Ottawa. Jesse hoped that by going back to where his life began he could begin the search for a better life.

Unfortunately, though, Jesse couldn't leave the leukemia behind.

Chapter Six

As Connor walked home from the hospital that evening, he couldn't help thinking how lucky he was to have a stepfather like Michael Kellaher. He couldn't imagine Michael ever raising his voice, let alone hitting or punching anyone – particularly Connor. He also recalled what Jesse had said about needing a bone marrow transplant in order to save his life. Jesse had told him that his chances of finding a bone marrow match within his family were almost impossible since his mother had died and he had no other family.

When Connor had asked him whether he had any aunts, uncles or cousins, Jesse had explained that his mother had been adopted and had left home when she was 16 – the same age as Jesse. Just before she died, Jesse's mother had told him her biggest regret was not reconnecting with her family for Jesse's sake.

When Connor arrived home that evening, he immediately went to the computer to find out more information about acute leukemia, chemotherapy and bone marrow transplants. He knew he could easily call Uncle Tim, his mother's brother, who was a doctor who specialized in diseases of the blood (or something like that). But he wanted to do this on his own. The more he researched the more he realized that Jesse's time was indeed running out. Now he understood what Jesse had undergone with his previous chemotherapy treatments. It sounded awful. He would have endured weekly visits to the hospital where deadly poison (for want of a better description) was injected into his veins in an effort to kill the cancer that invaded his blood. He would have lost weight, the ability to fight off infection and, of course, his hair. And to think that Jesse had endured chemotherapy twice, only to have the cancer return. It didn't seem fair.

As for a bone marrow transplant, Connor learned that there was something called the 'Bone Marrow Registry'. It contained the names and blood types of people from across the country and around the world. Anybody could donate a blood sample and anyone needing a bone marrow transplant could search the Registry through their medical doctor. If and when a match was found, that person could donate their bone marrow to save another's life. The Registry was a lifeline for those who could not find a family member who matched their blood and bone marrow type. In many cases, a sibling would provide the best opportunity for a match. A parent could be a match but it would not be as likely.

"Mum," called Connor, "come and see this!"

As his mother sat down next to him, he read aloud what he had found on the Internet about leukemia, chemotherapy and the purpose of the Bone Marrow Registry.

"Jesse told me that his only chance of surviving acute leukemia now is a bone marrow transplant. He has no family which means his only option is finding a match on the Registry," explained Connor. "I promised Jesse tonight that I'd try and help find him a bone marrow donor."

As usual, Fiona's emotions got the better of her and tears streamed down her cheeks.

"I'm so proud of you Connor," she said. "Michael, Frances come and hear what Connor has in mind to help Jesse."

Together, they worked out a plan. Connor would start by approaching Headmaster MacFarlane to ask whether he could organize a bone marrow donor drive for the Bone Marrow Registry at Worcester Academy. He was nervous, the following morning on his way to his first class, when stopped at the Headmaster's office to ask for an appointment to see him at noon. At the appointed hour, Connor smiled to himself as he approached Mrs. Simpson, the Headmaster's secretary. Coming to see Mr. MacFarlane on purpose seemed very funny to him.

"Good afternoon, Mrs. Simpson," said Connor, "I have an appointment with the Headmaster."

"He'll be right with you, Mr. Munro," replied Mrs. Simpson, as she pressed the intercom button to let Mr. MacFarlane know that his next appointment had arrived.

A few moments later, Headmaster MacFarlane appeared at his office door and signalled for Connor to join him. Timidly, Connor entered the office and waited for Mr. MacFarlane to sit before he took his own seat.

"Now, Mr. Munro, what can I do for you? It's not often that I have a student asking to see me on such short notice."

"Thank you very much for making time for me Headmaster," Connor began. "I have met a boy my age through the volunteer work that I'm doing at the Rideau Terrace homeless shelter. His name is Jesse and he's very sick with leukemia and will die without a bone marrow transplant. I told him, promised him actually, that I would try to help him find a donor. I was wondering whether you would give permission for a bone marrow donor drive to be held here at Worcester Academy. The purpose would be to ask potential bone marrow donors to come, give a sample of their blood and have it entered into something called the Bone Marrow Registry. If we're lucky, we might find a match for Jesse."

Mr. MacFarlane waited a few moments before he spoke. The silence seemed endless to Connor.

"Your request is a noble one, Mr. Munro. You are to be congratulated on your desire to help this young lad. I will have to seek approval from the Board of Governors, but I don't foresee any difficulty. I would ask that you prepare a one-page summary of your plan that I can present. Our next meeting is at the end of the week," said Mr. MacFarlane. As he stood, so too did Connor and the two shook hands.

"I'll have something to you by noon tomorrow, sir. Thank you for your encouragement and your confidence in me," said Connor as he left the office.

Connor rushed to the library to begin preparing the information sheet for the Headmaster's meeting with the Board of Governors. It hadn't even occurred to him that he'd missed his lunch hour.

Once seated at the computer in the library, Connor was stumped. He had no idea where to begin. He hadn't thought his plan through enough to realize that if he wanted it to succeed it meant a lot of work on his part. There had been other times in his short life when he had bitten off more than he could chew; promising to practise every day if he got an electric guitar; promising to work out regularly if he got weight-training equipment; and promising to walk it daily if he got a dog. The proof lay gathering dust on the guitar stand by his bed, gathering rust in the dumbbell rack in the basement and waiting patiently at the back door for a walk. This time was different, though. He was determined to keep his promise to Jesse.

At that moment, Frances came into the library to return a book. Connor motioned to her to come over. Even though she was a year behind him, he had to admit her reading and writing skills far outshone his own.

"Hey Connor," said Frances, "I don't think I've ever seen you in the library. What are you doing here?"

"I need your help."

"Why are you asking me, of all people, to help you?"

"'Cuz you're my sister and it's your job. Remember last night when I said I was going to help Jesse find a bone marrow donor?" Frances nodded. "Well, I just met with the Headmaster to ask if I could organize a bone marrow donor drive here. He wants me to write a page-long summary that explains what I want to do so that he can take it to his next meeting with the Board of Governors."

"I see. And you want me to write it for you. It'll cost you..."

"No, I want you to help me write it. Please, just give me some pointers."

"Okay, okay. Why don't you just write down the six questions that you always need to ask for a good story?"

"You know I have no idea what those are, Frances."

"They go like this: Who? What? When? Where? Why? and How? Once you've answered all those questions, your story will be written," said Frances, as she stood, patted Connor's shoulder, returned her book and left the library.

Connor took Frances' advice and began to write. It seemed as though the words just poured onto the computer screen. For once, he knew exactly what he wanted to say. When he had finished, he re-read his summary and was surprised at how well thought-out and convincing his plan was. He wondered what his mother would think. She'd always helped him with his book reports, projects and essays. He couldn't imagine what his marks would have been like without her intervention. This time, though, he was sure she wouldn't have to change much.

Chapter Seven

That evening when Connor arrived home from school, Fiona sensed that he'd had a good day. In some ways, Worcester Academy was hard on her son and it hurt her to see him struggle particularly with the social side of his school life. As Canada's capital, Ottawa was home to a large diplomatic corps; Ambassadors and High Commissioners from around the world whose sons and daughters attended Worcester Academy. The majority of the remainder of the student body comprised the offspring of Ottawa's ultra rich. They all lived in sprawling mansions within walking distance of the school. Yet, most of them arrived at Worcester every day in chauffeur-driven limousines.

Connor just didn't seem to fit in with either group. Fiona wondered whether he felt intimidated by them. His closest friends were those from his primary school days. Both Connor and Frances were invited regularly to parties and celebrations hosted by their Worcester friends, but sleepovers and their own birthdays were always filled with friends from what they called their 'old schools'.

Conversation around the dinner table focused on the day's highs and lows and Connor's meeting with Headmaster MacFarlane. When Frances mentioned that she had seen Connor in the library and had helped him with his summary, Fiona knew that this was the reason for Connor's good humour.

"Why don't you read your summary to us, Connor?" asked Fiona.

"Good idea, Fiona," replied Michael, "We'd love to hear it."

Connor didn't need any further persuasion. He left the table and retrieved his paper from his backpack. He cleared his throat and began to read what he had written. It was clear, sincere and amazingly grammatically correct. Spontaneous applause erupted – even Frances joined in.

"You liked it?" beamed Connor. "Let's hope the Board of Governors agrees with you."

"I can't see why they wouldn't," replied Fiona. "I think you'd better start planning that bone marrow donor drive right away."

"I'll take my paper to show Jesse after dinner," said Connor. "Some of the guys at the shelter pitched in to get him a card and they asked me to give it to him. You know, at first they kind of gave me the creeps but Mrs. Bradley says they're all just in an unfortunate situation."

That night, while soaking in the hot tub with her husband on the screened-in veranda gazing at the stars through the skylights, Fiona reflected on the change in Connor. She had to admit she hoped this interest and intensity would not be short-lived.

She also marvelled at the structure of Canada's health care system. Here was a boy with no home and no family and yet he had access to the best treatment medicine could offer – access that was equal to any other Canadian young or old, rich or poor.

Chapter Eight

The following Monday, Connor was called in to Headmaster MacFarlane's office to hear the Board's decision. As he entered the room, it was the Headmaster's turn to stand up, approach Connor and shake his hand.

"Congratulations, Mr. Munro, the Board unanimously agreed to your request. We're all behind you 100%. I'll write a letter today to the Canadian Blood Services requesting that a bone marrow donor drive be organized and set up here in the main gymnasium three weeks from today. Don't be surprised if there are certain steps we have to follow. For example, I imagine that any student under the age of 18 will have to have a consent form signed by their parents."

"Do you think they might say 'no'?"

"I would be very surprised if parents declined to give consent, particularly since the drive is being sanctioned by the Academy. Would you like to make your announcement at next week's school assembly?"

"Oh. I hadn't thought about that. I'm not very good at speaking in public. Couldn't I just put up some posters around the school?"

"Posters are a great idea, but I think you can paint a very clear and personal picture for everyone if you tell them about Jesse and how you came to meet and know him. As for speaking in public, it just takes practice and I have every confidence in you. "

"I'm glad one of us does!"

With that, Connor thanked the Headmaster and headed to his next class which happened to be his favourite - Art and Design.

He had no trouble writing and designing the poster for his upcoming bone marrow donor drive. He'd even given it a name – "The Big Match-Up". During art class, he designed a series of posters depending on who he wanted to reach and where he wanted to reach them - one for the teachers that talked about the importance of setting a good example (posted outside the teachers' lounge); one for the boys that stressed the importance of teamwork (posted outside the boys' locker room); and one for the girls that emphasized community spirit (posted outside the cafeteria). Connor's mother was always talking about "target audiences" and "key messages" when she described her work to people. Now he understood what she meant and he would soon see how well they worked.

Once the posters were up in their designated spots, it didn't take long for teachers, staff and students to approach Connor with questions and offers of help. His apprehension about how his plan would be received at Worcester Academy soon eased and he found himself looking forward to speaking at the next assembly.

One person in particular who offered to help Connor was the daughter of the American Ambassador to Canada. Lindsay Giffen was a tall, blond, blue-eyed southern belle from Georgia nicknamed 'Lovely Lindsay'. To Connor, she was a vision of perfection and he worshipped her from afar. He'd never spoken to her, never even uttered her name out loud and now here she was, Lovely Lindsay, standing in front of him with tears in her eyes saying his name.

"Connor, you are my total hero!" she said in her distinctive southern drawl. "I'd love to be involved in your donor drive. There's always some kind of special event being organized at my house so please let me know if there is anything I can do to help. Are you alright, Connor, you seem a little dazed," Lindsay added as she waved her hand in front of his face.

After a slight pause, Connor realized he wasn't dreaming and that he had to respond. As usual, he started with, "Umm…, thanks Lindsay, I could use some help. I'm a bit overwhelmed by the response."

"Well, maybe I could meet you after school and make a list of what needs to get done. We've only got a few weeks to get the word out to as many people as possible."

"That's a great idea, but I volunteer at a homeless shelter after school. That's where I met Jesse. It's about four blocks from here, on the corner of Beachwood and Birch. Hey, maybe you could meet me there we could start putting together a 'to-do' list."

"I know exactly where it is. I'll meet you there!"

As Lindsay turned and walked away, Connor couldn't help but watch her shiny blond hair sway in time with her footsteps. Had she really stopped to talk to him? Had she really offered to help him? He still wasn't completely convinced. If she showed up at the shelter later, he'd know for sure.

The rest of the school day crawled by and finally Connor arrived at the shelter to begin his shift. He was just getting the telephone message pad ready when in walked Lindsay dressed in 'street' clothes. He'd never seen her in anything other than her school uniform and he couldn't believe she could look any more beautiful but she did.

She smiled brightly when she saw Connor and came right up and dropped her backpack on the desk. "Hey Connor, I brought lots of paper, pens, highlighters and a calendar to get us going. Is there another chair around? You won't get into trouble if I sit with you behind the desk?"

Again Connor was dumbfounded. She actually came. Their conversation earlier in the day hadn't been an hallucination after all.

"No one will mind that you're here, Lindsay," he replied. "They all know Jesse and are grateful that I'm trying to help him. A few of them will come out here after they've finished their dinner to see how I'm doing. I hope that's okay with you because when I first started the people here made me very nervous and uncomfortable. But now I realize that they just need some understanding and support."

"I don't mind," said Lindsay, "Back home in Savannah, my mother and I volunteered at a home for mentally handicapped adults. That's why I called you my hero because I know what it means to want to help someone who doesn't have the same opportunities as we do. Now, before we get started on our list, I would like to know how you met Jesse."

Once Connor had finished telling Lindsay about Jesse, he understood, through the questions she asked and the comments she made, that she genuinely shared his commitment to find a bone marrow donor in order to save Jesse's life. They then started planning The Big Match-Up.

Chapter Nine

When Fiona picked up Connor that evening from the shelter, he strode to the car with new-found confidence and a wide smile. She knew he had big news. She could read him like a book. He was hopeless at telling lies; the truth was always written all over his face.

"You look like you're in a good mood," said Fiona.

"Mum, you won't believe it! The prettiest girl in the school wants to help me with the donor drive. She said I was her hero. We've put together a 'to-do' list. She's amazing. Her name is Lindsay and her Mum is the American Ambassador. Did I tell you she said I was her hero?" said Connor all in one breath.

"I see. So I guess that means the meeting with Headmaster MacFarlane went well?"

"More than well. The Board of Governors agreed to my request and I put up posters all around the school. The response has been amazing! Everyone was stopping me in the hall and asking all about it. Headmaster MacFarlane has asked me to make an announcement at the next school assembly."

"What terrific news. We'll give you all the help you need."

That night after dinner, the entire family poured over Connor's 'to-do' list. With only three weeks to go before The Big Match-Up, there were so many things on the list that they decided to divide it up and each take responsibility for the various tasks. Frances volunteered to write all the different texts that could be used in letters or emails to potential donors. There would be one for parents, one for businesses in the area, one for principals at other high schools (challenging them to match or better Worcester's student turn-out) and one for the diplomatic community that surrounded Worcester Academy.

Fiona would prepare all the distribution lists for the letters and emails and would then send them either via snail mail or electronically. Michael volunteered to do what he did best – get the word out. He'd make calls to his colleagues in the media to see if they might be interested in covering the event. He was certain a story like this would have legs and would strike a chord with many a journalist who may have faced a life-altering diagnosis within their own family. Fiona knew he'd tackle it first thing in the morning.

Her next task was to get Connor started on his presentation for next week's school assembly. But he was way ahead of her. Before she knew it, he was at his desk unfolding and smoothing out papers full of ideas and suggestions that he and Lindsay had come up with at the shelter. He started with the obvious – introducing himself and telling the student body why he was up on stage.

Taking his mother's advice, he would keep it short, to the point and not too technical. He didn't want his school-mates' eyes to glaze over like they did in Miss Roberts' chemistry class when she endeavoured to explain the difference between acidic and alkaline solutions or when Mr. Saunders pontificated in English class about Lady Macbeth's obsession about clean hands.

His research into leukemia and bone marrow transplants had taught him there were two types: autologous which uses the patient's own bone marrow and allogenic which uses bone marrow from a donor, usually a brother or sister. If there is no sibling, as in Jesse's case, a search of tissue-typed volunteers could be made to find a matched but unrelated donor. All of this sounded very positive; however, Connor knew it would be like finding a needle in a haystack. Discovering a match for Jesse would take a miracle.

Fiona suggested that Connor project a photograph or two of Jesse during his presentation to help everyone see that Jesse was just like they were and that this disease could easily happen to someone in their family. Connor liked the idea and would bring a camera to the hospital on his next visit with Jesse. Working late into the night, he finally completed his presentation and felt a certain satisfaction that he could really make a difference in Jesse's life.

Chapter 10

At breakfast the next morning, Connor was excited to show off his presentation. He rushed into the kitchen waving sheets of paper and said, "I finished my presentation last night. Maybe tonight after dinner I could practise it."

"Sure, Connor," said Fiona, "we could be your test audience."

"And I've started the letters," said Frances. "Could you look them over tonight, Dad?"

"By all means, Frances," replied Michael. "And Connor, you'd better get your game face on and have your TV makeup handy because I think you'll be doing some interviews very shortly."

"Get out! Do you really think so?"

"I sure do. How do you think Jesse would react to being asked for an interview?"

"Gee, I don't know. It's hard to read him sometimes. I could ask him tonight when I visit the hospital."

As they drove into work together, Fiona asked Michael whether he thought Connor was getting in over his head with Jesse and the donor drive. She was worried that it might all be too much for both boys and that there would be such disappointment if no donor was found to be a match for Jesse.

"You know what Connor is like, Michael, when things don't work out the way he expects them to. He'll get discouraged and we'll be left do deal with his long face and can't-do attitude."

"Normally I would agree with you, Fiona, but I think he's changed over the last couple of weeks. I can't quite put my finger on it, but he seems determined to do what he can to help Jesse and I'm convinced he knows it's a long shot to find a perfect donor. If anything, the whole experience will give him confidence – we've seen that already – and show him that even one person can make a difference."

She loved the daily drive into work. Ottawa was a beautiful city and being the capital of the country meant that much was spent on keeping it that way. Although they lived in the suburbs, it never took more than fifteen minutes to get downtown. Their route took them along the Rideau Canal. Built as protection against the threat of American attack, it opened in 1832. Construction was supervised by Colonel John By, hence Ottawa's original name "Bytown", and it connected the city of Ottawa, on the Ottawa River with the city of Kingston, 100 miles south, on Lake Ontario. Funnily enough, once the Rideau Canal was completed, no further military disputes erupted between the two countries. Now it was used strictly for pleasure – boating in the spring, summer and fall and skating in the winter.

Along the Canal as it runs through Ottawa, meanders Colonel By Drive on the East side and Queen Elizabeth Drive on the West. There are no traffic lights and no stop signs; just borders of immaculately manicured lawns and flowerbeds. Even though fall was fast approaching, there was still a riot of colour throughout the flowerbeds. Each year, just before the first frost, teams of landscapers descend on these gardens. They meticulously remove all the plants and prepared the beds for winter.

One of Ottawa's claims to fame is its annual Tulip Festival, held during the month of May – the largest outside Holland. It started with a gift of one hundred thousand tulip bulbs from Princess Juliana of the Netherlands after the end of the Second World War. She gave Canada the bulbs to say thank you for the safe haven that she and her family received in Ottawa during the occupation of Holland and in recognition of the role Canadian soldiers played in her country's liberation. During her family's stay in Ottawa, Princess Juliana's daughter,

Princess Margriet, was born at the Civic Hospital. In order to ensure that the new Princess would carry Dutch citizenship, thereby also ensuring her eligibility to inherit the Dutch crown, the hospital's Board of Governors and the Canadian Government arranged to have Princess Juliana's maternity room temporarily declared international territory.

Fiona smiled as she recalled with pride the pivotal role her maternal grandfather, as Chairman of the hospital's Board of Directors, had played in drafting that declaration. The initial gift of one hundred thousand tulip bulbs had grown exponentially as the Dutch Government continued to send bulbs each year. Now, during the first three weeks of May, hundreds of thousands of tulips bloom simultaneously. Thousands of tourists flock to Ottawa annually to marvel at the wide ribbons of red, yellow, purple, orange and pink as far as the eye can see along both sides of the Canal.

Throughout the day, Michael either popped his head into Fiona's office or sent her quick emails updating her on his progress with pitching Connor's story to the media. He was having great success. All the local outlets, both print and electronic, were keenly interested and would definitely attend the donor drive at Worcester Academy. A number were even interested in giving the event some advance coverage. As the date drew nearer, he would cast his net further afield across the country to see if he could drum up interest at the national level.

Fiona concentrated on developing lists of those who to whom she could send a letter of invitation to attend the donor drive. She called the staff together – twelve heads were always better than one. While most company presidents might use the telephone or the email to call a staff meeting or a brainstorming session in the boardroom, Fiona stood at the boardroom doors and rang an antique school bell. At the sound of the distinctive clanging, the staff appeared in the hallway and proceeded to the boardroom. Whenever Hamilton and Kellaher won a new piece of business, the bell was used to 'ring in' the new client. However, the bell's use had been since been expanded to call the staff together for announcements, birthdays and general displays of excitement.

After Fiona had told her staff the story about Connor, Jesse and the planned bone marrow donor drive, there was silence, followed by an enthusiastic round of applause. Then the suggestions started flying. She barely had time to write them all down on the flip chart. At the end of the day, her staff presented her with a ten-page, colour-coded spread sheet, complete with names, titles, street and email addresses and phone numbers – all sorted by type and location of business, school or profession. Her staff had even volunteered their time to follow up with key contacts on the list to ensure maximum turnout at the donor drive. Most of them had known Connor since he was in Kindergarten and would do all they could to see him succeed.

Chapter 11

At lunch, Connor met up with Frances and Lindsay, in the cafeteria, to review the to-do list, Frances' letters and Connor's notes for his presentation. Connor introduced his sister to Lindsay and the first words out of her mouth were, "Are you guys twins?"

"We get that a lot," said Connor as Frances rolled her eyes, "We're not even related!"

"Boy, y'all could have fooled me," said Lindsay as she fished out her copy of the to-do list from her binder, "Guess what? I talked to my Mama about the donor drive last night and her face lit up like the fourth of July. She offered to call all her diplomat friends in the neighbourhood. She showed me the phone list and there must be a hundred of them on it!"

"That's really nice of her, Lindsay," said Connor, "we could give her the letter that Frances has written so that she'd have all the information to tell them over the phone. Do you think they would want a formal invitation?"

"Y'all don't know my mother," replied Lindsay. "She can charm the spots off a hog. She'll have all those people promising to come and to bring two friends!"

"Your Mum sounds like a hoot, Lindsay," said Frances.

"Speaking of invitations," said Lindsay reaching into her satchel, "my mother asked me to give you this one for your stepmother. She's hosting a luncheon for the Women's Business Network and guess what – you're invited too! It's a mother-daughter-power-of-women thing."

"Fiona will go for sure! She's all about young women having role models and mentors. I guess you'll be there to?" replied Frances.

"Do you think I have a choice?" said Lindsay, laughing.

"I forgot to tell you," interjected Connor, "my Mum suggested that we show some photos of Jesse during my presentation. So when I visit him after dinner tonight I'll bring a camera. Hey, Lindsay, why don't you come home with us for dinner and then we could walk over to the hospital? It's just across the street from us."

"I'd like that," replied Lindsay. "Do you think Jesse would mind? What about your parents? I can't just show up for dinner."

"You leave Jesse to me," said Connor, "and as for our parents, we bring friends home all the time for dinner – they're cool with it."

"That's right," said Frances. "Fiona just puts another potato in the pot or adds another layer on the lasagne."

"Well, I'll have to clear it with HQ and the secret service," said Lindsay, "but there shouldn't be a problem. All I need is your address and we can all go in the embassy limo instead of the 72-seat variety that y'all normally take home." They all had a good chuckle over Lindsay's joke and as she wrote down the address they agreed to meet at the drop-off circle at the end of the school day.

There were four Houses at Worcester Academy. After registering at the school, students were assigned to houses, based on academic interests, athletic strengths, artistic capabilities and family connections. Connor and Frances, since they were siblings, were assigned to Macdonald House, named after Canada's first Prime Minister, Sir John A. Macdonald. As luck would have it, Lindsay was also in Mac House. Throughout the school year, students would be expected to win points for their respective houses by excelling at sporting events, science fairs, music festivals, art exhibitions and community spirit. The house that garnered the most points at the end of the year would win bragging rights and the school banner. Connor's planned donor drive was sure to win points for Mac House – or so he hoped.

At the end of the day Connor, Lindsay and Frances waited at the drop-off circle for the embassy limo to pick them up. Sure enough, after a couple of minutes, up rolled a long, black, shiny limousine with tinted windows and American eagles bolted to the doors. The telltale red license plates with white lettering denoted the car's link to the diplomatic community – a familiar sight throughout the city. As the driver-side window was lowered, Lindsay said, "Hello Mr. Abbott. Did y'all get my mother's message about my invitation to have dinner at my friend Connor's house?"

At that moment Connor noticed the chauffeur wasn't the only person in the front seat. Beside him sat a large, burly man with a buzz cut and a face that could stop traffic. This must be the secret service agent Lindsay had mentioned. He couldn't imagine being watched by someone all the time; having to ask everyone's permission simply to go to a friend's house. As the daughter of the American Ambassador to Canada, though, he understood the danger Lindsay could be in if someone decided to kidnap her as a way of demanding retribution from or retaliating against something that they thought the United States had done to them.

"Yes, Miss Lindsay, we got your message," said the chauffeur. "In you get and we'll be off to Faircrest Heights."

The limousine slid effortlessly into the rush-hour traffic and in no time at all they arrived at the Hamilton-Kellaher residence. Connor loved to bring new friends home. He liked to see the expression on their faces when they first drove into the circular drive. Their house was truly a one-of-a-kind, based on the famous American architect Frank Lloyd Wright's pagoda design. He'd heard his Mum tell the story many times as she took guests on the mandatory guided tour. The house was constructed in the early 1960s by a local Ottawa commercial real estate developer. Built entirely, inside and out, from white marble imported from Georgia and accented with western red cedar and mahogany, the story was that the contractor went bankrupt building the house because of all the design changes and rejected materials by the developer's wife.

The end result, though, was an architectural marvel. True to Frank Lloyd Wright style, elements of the outside of the house flowed naturally to the inside, like the marble walls, the terrazzo steps and landings as well as the western red cedar. Lloyd's use of expansive, apex-shaped windows at the front and back of the house flooded it with light throughout the year. Even in the dead of winter, the ambient light in the house betrayed even the darkest days outside.

A repeating motif – another architectural feature typically found in a Frank Lloyd Wright design – was incorporated into every part of the house, from the fence enclosing the back of the property, to the front and garage doors, to the floor-to-ceiling lattice work in the front hall, to the shoji-screen doors between the den and the sunken living room, to the door handles of the vestibules. It was even appliquéd onto the front of the basement wet-bar (a typical feature in 1960s homes), woven into one of the bedroom carpets and etched into the glass door of the shower in the master bathroom.

Connor particularly liked viewing the house from the outside at night, with the inside recessed lights on because it glowed like a delicate Japanese lantern. The roof appeared to rest precariously on clerestory windows that ringed its perimeter. The walls in the living room were covered with turquoise and gold silk and those in the "Liberace" bathroom – so called because of its lavishness and because Liberace had actually visited the house – were dressed with gold and black velvet wallpaper.

The best thing that Connor loved about his house was that it was a party palace. The basement went on forever and could accommodate loud music, video games, air hockey tournaments, darts, pool and multi-person sleep-overs. Of course, the hot tub was also a popular party activity.

As they piled out of the limousine, Connor thanked the chauffeur and asked whether Lindsay would be allowed to walk to the Children's Hospital after dinner. The chauffer made it clear that the car would wait in the driveway until

Lindsay was ready to return home and he would to check to see whether she would be permitted to go to the hospital but he knew she certainly would not be permitted to walk there. The bodyguard nodded in agreement.

With that, Connor and the two girls climbed the front steps and went inside. "We're home and we've brought a friend for dinner," called Connor as they opened the front doors to the foyer.

"That's great," replied Fiona from the kitchen, "we're having burritos, guacamole and salad. I hope that's okay with everyone. Come on in and start setting the table, please."

Frances headed down the hall to put her backpack in her room while Connor led Lindsay into the kitchen to meet his mother and stepfather. "Mum and Michael, I'd like you to meet Lindsay. She's been helping me with the donor drive and she's in Mac House. She's from Georgia and her Mum's the American Ambassador."

"Very pleased to meet you, Lindsay," said Fiona as they shook hands. You're Chloe Giffen's daughter. I heard your mother speak the other day at a business women's luncheon. She's doing a terrific job."

"Thank you for your kind words, ma'am. It's so nice to meet you," said Lindsay, "and I'd also like to thank you for your hospitality. Connor gave me every assurance that it wouldn't be an imposition if I showed up unannounced."

"He's responsible for setting the extra place at the table and for doing the extra dishes," said Michael as he too shook Lindsay's hand, "and we get the added benefit of enjoying your company. So I think we come out ahead of the game."

"We rode home in the embassy limousine," said Connor, "It's parked in the driveway with the chauffeur and the bodyguard just waiting for Lindsay. Pretty cool, eh?"

"Is there anything I can do to help, sir?" Lindsay asked Michael.

"You can start by calling us Fiona and Michael, if you'd like," he replied.

"That's kind of you to offer, sir, but I'd be in a whole heap of trouble if my parents found out. In Georgia, we're taught from the cradle to say 'yes, sir' and 'no, ma'am', no matter what the circumstance."

"Are you listening, Connor?" said Fiona, "You see, you're not the only one who's learning good manners and social etiquette from their parents."

Connor feigned exasperation and finished setting the table.

Dinner conversation revolved around the donor drive and what had been accomplished that day. Michael promised Frances that he would go over the letters she had written and Connor asked if he could borrow the digital camera to take pictures of Jesse that evening when he and Lindsay visited him at the hospital. Frances mentioned the mother-daughter luncheon invitation from Ambassador Giffen and, true to Frances' prediction, Fiona said she wouldn't miss it for the world. Lindsay regaled them with stories about her life in Savannah and about her first experience with snow and frigid temperatures in Ottawa. Music, she told them, was her passion – the piano in particular. She'd been playing since she was six and had competed in many national and international piano festivals. When Fiona suggested Lindsay play a little something for them after dinner, she beamed.

"I hope you won't be disappointed in our piano, Lindsay. It's only an old Steinway studio grand," said Fiona with a wink.

"It would be a privilege to play such a fine instrument. Is it a family heirloom?"

"Yes it is. It belonged to my grandfather, then to my mother and now to me."

"Do you play?"

"In a manner of speaking, yes I do."

"Well, then, maybe we could play a duet or two, sometime."

"You're on, Lindsay!"

As Connor and Frances cleared the table and put dishes away, Lindsay serenaded them with a selection of classical and contemporary pieces. She certainly was talented, Connor thought and he suddenly wished he'd taken more of an interest in his mother's abilities as a pianist. After a round of hearty applause, Connor and Lindsay put together a 'CARE' package for Jesse, retrieved the camera from the hall closet and headed out the front door to the waiting limousine. They jumped into the back seat and Lindsay asked whether it was alright for her to go with Connor to the Children's Hospital. The chauffeur responded with a 'thumbs-up' and the bodyguard nodded ever so slightly. The latter had still not uttered a single word and Connor wanted to make a comment to Lindsay about it but didn't dare. He'd seen too many movies about gun-toting secret service, FBI and CIA agents who'd shoot first and ask questions later. He hadn't seen this one talk into his shirt cuff, though and he couldn't detect the requisite ear piece. Connor was about to ask whether the chauffeur needed directions but the car turned left out of the circular drive and then immediately right onto the street that brought them to the entrance to the Children's Hospital.

"You weren't kidding when you said the hospital was across the street from your house, Connor," said Lindsay. The limo dropped the pair at the main entrance and Connor told the chauffeur they would return in half an hour, since visiting hours would be over then.

As they proceeded to the bank of elevators, Lindsay asked, "Do you think Jesse will mind that I'm coming with you?"

"I don't think so," replied Connor, "It must be very lonely lying there all day staring at the ceiling, waiting for someone to come and poke you with a needle or bring you a tray of the most unappetizing-looking food."

They reached his room and went straight in. Jesse was sitting up, listening to the Walkman and smiled when he saw Connor. The smile faded when it registered with Jesse that Connor was not alone. "Who's this?" asked Jesse suspiciously.

"This is my friend, Lindsay," said Connor. "She's helping me with your donor drive. I'm sorry I didn't let you know she was coming, but it was a spur-of-the-moment thing."

"If y'all would rather I waited out in the hall, I completely understand," said Lindsay.

"Say what?" asked Jesse as he raised one eyebrow and cocked his head to one side, "You have the funniest way of talking. You're not from around here, are you?"

"No, I'm from Savannah, Georgia. But I go to Connor's school here."

"No kidding," said Jesse as his smile returned and filled his whole face. "Connor, you dog, where have you been hiding her?"

"Down, boy," said Connor, "or else the dials on those machines are going to set off an alarm or something. We brought you magazines, chips, juice and tapes. And we'd like to take some pictures of you and me so that I can show them at the school assembly next week during my presentation about the donor drive."

"Hey, if Lindsay wants to take pictures of me, who am I to argue," said Jesse with a wink.

Connor was relieved Jesse didn't mind that he'd brought Lindsay, but his coming on to her didn't sit well with him. He took the camera out of his pocket, gave it to Lindsay, sat on the bed next to Jesse and scowled at the camera.

"Okay, I want to see faces as round as a big ol' Georgia peach!" said Lindsay.

That made them both smile and Lindsay took a number of shots and then asked a nurse to take some of the three of them together.

The rest of their time was spent talking about all the things that needed to happen before the donor drive and that the news media might be interested in the story. "We might even get asked to be interviewed," said Connor.

"Cool," replied Jesse, "My stepfather always said I'd end up on TV but then he'd add 'on America's Most Wanted'. It would be great for him to see me on the news doing something good. And speaking of doing good things, Connor, there's something I've been meaning to tell you. I know it was your Walkman that we stole that day on the bus. I've known it from the first day I saw you standing at the end of the bed. I just haven't had the guts to tell you how sorry I am and to give it back." Jesse reached over to the bedside table and handed the Walkman to Connor.

Connor shook his head and said, "I'd like you to keep it. If it hadn't been for that Walkman, none of this would have happened and I'm glad it did."

"So am I," replied Jesse as he lay back and closed his eyes. Connor sensed Jesse was close to tears and was moved that his new friend felt comfortable enough to express his true feelings. Lindsay, too, could feel the raw emotion and reached into her pocket for a tissue.

Connor and Lindsay could see Jesse was tiring and helped him get settled for the night. They said their goodbyes and headed out the door. The limousine pulled up just as the two arrived at the hospital's front doors. Both Connor and Lindsay were absorbed in their own thoughts as the driver dropped Connor off at home. Lindsay waved out the window as the limo headed down the street. Connor wondered whether he should have given her a kiss but quickly dismissed the idea as ill-conceived. He pictured the two men in the front seat not taking too kindly to his romantic advance on their charge. Maybe the next time they were alone ... Who was he kidding? He'd probably never have the courage to give Lindsay anything but a hug.

Chapter 12

The rest of the week was filled with practices – Frances' rugby and Connor's presentation. The Worcester Academy girls' rugby team was the best in the city and had won the provincial championship two years in a row. The team had been invited to an international rugby tournament in Rome in six week's time. Frances was vying for the chance to play scrum half. There were three girls in the running for the position. Frances was the youngest player on the team but by far the most passionate and, according to her parents, the most talented.

Fiona would never forget watching Frances' first rugby game. Unfamiliar with the sport, there were times when Fiona had to hide behind her husband in order to shield herself from its roughness. She was shocked at the intensity of the play and the sheer physical force that these young women displayed. At the end of the game, Frances ran to greet her parents on the sidelines – skinned knees, bruised shins and mud-caked elbows proudly displayed. She removed her mouthguard (her only article of protective gear), spat a mouthful of dirt on the grass and, with a huge grin on her face, proclaimed that rugby was the best sport ever!

Connor ran through his presentation a number of times with Fiona who gave him pointers on how to remain calm, focused but most of all sincere and, hopefully, inspiring. The photographs that Lindsay took at the hospital were terrific. Connor incorporated them into a PowerPoint deck along with key facts and information about leukemia, Jesse's life and the steps involved in donating a blood sample for the bone marrow drive. He then timed the slides to change according to his speaking notes.

The morning of the presentation to the school assembly, Connor woke refreshed and eager to start the day. His mother had offered to drive him and his sister to school so he would have time to read his notes once more. On the way to school, Fiona kept the conversation light so that Connor wouldn't arrive a bundle of nerves but she needn't have worried. He was confident and in fact looking forward to his stage debut.

With a sound and equipment check complete, Connor waited backstage with the Headmaster for the students to take their seats. The familiar murmuring and sporadic outbursts of laughter reached Connor's ears as he watched Headmaster MacFarlane proceed to the podium and call for quiet. He gave the students an overview of why they had been called to the assembly and then gave Connor the floor. The auditorium was silent. Connor stepped up to the podium as the lights dimmed.

"Thank you Headmaster MacFarlane," Connor began. "Good morning fellow students. My name is Connor Munro and I'm not facing a death sentence. But I'd like you to meet someone who is."

He then took them on a factual journey through the disease called leukemia and the havoc it wreaks on the body. He spoke slowly, emphatically and passionately as he described the various stages of the disease, its death rate and the available treatment options. He then paused and let a photo of Jesse fill the screen behind him. "There is only one option left for the person you see here," he continued, "and that's a bone marrow transplant."

As he described how he met Jesse and how his story had affected him, the outpouring of compassion from his fellow students was palpable. He went on to give the details about the donor drive to be held at the school and the fact that Worcester was about to issue a challenge to other high schools to match the number of student donors they could muster at the drive. With that, a cheer rippled through the auditorium followed by a standing ovation and the raucous singing of the Worcester Academy fight song.

Connor was on cloud nine. Lindsay found him in the crowd as they all exited the auditorium and headed to their classes. She gave him a Georgia-sized hug and told him how proud she was to know him. Connor had never heard talk like that from someone his own age and somehow it meant more to him than when his parents told him the same thing.

The day flew by as did the rest of the week. Now that the wheels were in motion for the donor drive, life returned to normal for Connor. He signed up for the first of his driver's ED classes and registered for house league hockey. Mid-terms were coming up fast as were the deadlines for book reports and history papers. He'd already completed half the required volunteer hours at the homeless shelter and his visits with Jesse came as a pleasant break from his studies.

Jesse was getting stronger although the disease was still very much alive in his blood. Connor was able to get Jesse to talk more about himself and what he'd been through in his short life. He could sense, though, Jesse's reluctance to wish for a bone marrow donor match and he certainly didn't want to get Jesse's hopes up.

Chapter 13

The day of the donor drive, the Canadian Blood Services transformed the main gymnasium into twenty donor stations, staffed by nurses who would take the blood samples. At nine o'clock sharp, the doors to the gym opened and the line that had formed down the hall, around the corner and into the cafeteria began to move.

Connor was the first to roll up his sleeve, even though he had a severe aversion to needles. A tourniquet was applied to his upper arm. The nurse tightened it and tapped his vein at the bend in his elbow. "Nice and plump," she said. "Just what I like to see."

She swabbed the area with disinfectant and said, "Now, make a nice tight fist for me. I'm going to insert the needle on the count of three. You'll feel just a little sting."

Connor closed his eyes and held his breath. After the nurse counted to three, he felt a slight prick of the needle. She loosened the tourniquet told him to relax his fist. She filled three vials of his blood in less than thirty seconds, removed the needle and placed a small piece of cotton batten at the site and told Connor to press down on it. After a couple of minutes, she removed the cotton batten and placed a small, round Band-Aid over the needle mark. By this time, he'd opened his eyes and was amazed to see not only that it was all over, but also that the gym was filled to capacity with donors.

His research about bone marrow transplants had taught Connor that bone marrow is a pulpy tissue found inside long bones such as the ribs, pelvis or breastbone and could be compared to a factory where red and white blood cells, as well as platelets were made. A bone marrow donor provides the replacement marrow used in a transplant. Donors and patients are matched according to the compatibility of genetic markers called Human Leukocyte Antigens, or HLA, inherited from your parents. A minimum of 12 of these antigens are considered essential in order for the donor to be considered a match. That sounded like a lot to Connor and even though it looked as though there would be hundreds of donors at his drive, he knew it would still be like looking for a needle in a haystack.

On his way out of the gym he met Lindsay. She was standing in line with her mother. "Hi Connor," she said. "I'm glad I saw you before class. Mama, this is Connor."

"It's an honour to meet you Ambassador Giffen," said Connor as he extended his hand.

"The honour is all mine, I assure you, Connor," replied the Ambassador as she shook his hand warmly. "Lindsay has told me all about your mission to help a friend in need. I find your actions truly admirable."

"What was it like to have your blood taken? Did it hurt? Were you nervous?" asked Lindsay.

"A piece of cake," said Connor. "Don't worry about a thing." There was no way he was going to admit how nervous he'd been.

At noon, ten school buses arrived at Worcester Academy and students poured from the doors like water from a tap. Connor and Lindsay threw open the big oak doors to greet them. Two hundred students from three neighbouring high schools had risen to Worcester's challenge.

Shortly after the students arrived, so too did reporters from local as well as national television and radio networks, newspapers and wire services. Fiona and Michael, both having completed their blood donations, were on hand to brief the reporters, guide them to the gymnasium for photo ops and, most importantly, stay by Connor's side, just out of camera range, as he granted interview after interview. Fiona was amazed at Connor's apparent ease in front of the cameras and microphones. He was putting to good use all the interview 'dos and don'ts' she had taught him. Gone was his habitual sentence opener, "Ummm..", as well as his tendency to shrug his shoulders and look down at the floor. Instead, he gave heart-felt, information-filled, six-second sound bites; any shorter and the answer would be lacking in substance; any longer and the answer would be lost on the audience.

By the end of the day, Canadian Blood Services had confirmed that 500 donors had been processed. Headmaster MacFarlane asked Connor to make the announcement over the PA system from the main office. Loud cheering and desk banging greeted the news. Connor went on to thank all Worcester students and parents who agreed to donate their blood. He also announced that the 200 students from Immaculata High School, Glebe Collegiate and Lisgar Collegiate provided the biggest boost to the drive. More cheering rang through the halls. He saved his last thanks for Headmaster MacFarlane and Worcester's Board of Governors for having granted permission to hold the donor drive at the school and to let the students take time from their classes to volunteer. Connor ended by stating that his belief in volunteerism had been reaffirmed, having witnessed it full force throughout the day.

He couldn't wait to get to the hospital to tell Jesse the good news. He got off the bus as usual but instead of heading home, he ran straight there. Out of breath, Connor reached Jesse's bedside and exclaimed, "We had 500 donors show up today, Jesse. Can you believe it?"

Jesse shrugged in response. "Didn't you hear what I said?" asked Connor.

"Yeah, I heard you."

"Is that all you can say?"

"What do you want, a hero badge?"

"I thought you'd be stoked."

"It still doesn't mean I won't die."

"I know that, but at least it will give you a fighting chance."

"A chance for what? They're releasing me from the hospital at the end of the week. What chance do I have with no home and no family?"

And there it was; the reason for Jesse's complete lack of enthusiasm. "My whole life," Jesse continued, "I've been promised things that never come true. Now that the donor drive is over, you'll find something else to keep you busy – Lindsay for instance. I've given up wishing for anything good to happen 'cuz then when things go down the shitter – and they always do - it won't make any difference to me. And stop looking at me like that."

Connor was stung. How could Jesse think that he would abandon him? "I can't help looking at you like this," Connor said. "If you think I'm giving up on you after all the hard work I've put in, you'd better think again. Look, I know you haven't had much luck with people watching your back but I am, trust me!"

With that remark, Jesse just rolled his eyes, crossed his arms and said, "Like I've never heard that one before." It was as if he couldn't let himself believe that a relative stranger was willing to help him with no strings attached. His body language and facial expression suggested distain for Connor and all he had – a sheltered life filled with a loving family, friends and material possessions; a far cry from Jesse's life in a shelter of a much different sort.

"I've got a good feeling about the donor drive," said Connor. "Let's just take it one day at a time and see what happens. Like, where will you go when they spring you from here?"

"Dunno. Probably back to my street family, I guess. The weather's still warm enough to sleep outside."

Connor knew better than to chastise Jesse, even though it was certain that Jesse's health would worsen if he didn't take better care of himself. Connor wondered how the doctors could release him when they knew he had nowhere to go. It didn't make any sense. What did make sense was for Jesse to stay with Connor at his house. He would just have to devise a plan that would have Jesse making the suggestion and thinking the idea was all his.

Chapter 14

As Connor walked up the driveway, he could see his mother through the kitchen window having an animated conversation on the telephone. She waved and then motioned to him to pick up the pace.

"Quick, Connor," Fiona said as he opened the door, "it's Uncle Tim on the phone. He's just seen you on the news and he wants to speak with you."

"Hi Uncle Tim," said Connor. "Yup, that was me." The rest of the conversation was one-sided, as Fiona could hear only Connor's responses to her brother's questions and comments. Dr. Tim Hamilton, her older brother by three years, was a professor at the University of Toronto and the country's leading haematologist. He was also a much sought-after speaker on the international stage by those wishing to hear the latest breakthroughs on and treatments for blood-borne and blood-related diseases. In his 'spare' time, he wrote medical mysteries and was currently ranked fourth on the New York Times Best Sellers List for his latest novel aptly titled *Blood is Thickest in Water.*

"Thanks, Uncle Tim, I will," Connor said and then hung up the phone.

"Well," said Fiona, "what did he say?"

"He said he saw me on the 6 o'clock news and that I looked and sounded better than most of his colleagues when they get interviewed."

"I told you. You're a natural! We're taping as many of the television and radio interviews as we can and we'll get copies of the print articles tomorrow."

"I'm glad the hospital said no to the reporters interviewing Jesse. He was not in a good mood. He's afraid I'm going to forget all about him now that the donor drive is over. I can't believe they're releasing him from the hospital on Friday. They're such idiots. They know he has nowhere to go. You should see him, Mum, he's really discouraged."

Connor was about to broach the subject of Jesse coming to stay with them when his mother said, "I've been thinking about that. In fact I've made a call or two to the Children's Aid Society and to the Children's Hospital."

As usual, his mother was one step ahead of him. "I told them about Jesse," she continued, "and the first question they asked me was how old is he. Do you know if he's fifteen or sixteen, because it makes quite a difference to the CAS?"

"He told me he's sixteen but I haven't seen a birth certificate or anything. Why is his age a big deal?"

"Because, if he's under sixteen and has a parent who could take care of him, he should go back to that parent. But if that parent is unable or unwilling to care for him, he would be placed in foster care. Now, if Jesse is sixteen, the Children's Aid Society has no legal jurisdiction over him and he may decide where he lives."

"I get it! So that means all we have to do is convince Jesse that the best decision for him is to stay here. Our only problem is that if I suggest it, he'll say 'no' for sure."

"You have until the end of the week to plant the seed, hon," said Fiona. What she didn't tell Connor was that both the CAS and the Children's Hospital had told her to be very careful. Typically, homeless teenagers were masters of manipulation, they said. Lying, stealing and vandalism were the hallmarks of their trade. They warned Fiona not to put herself or her family at risk and to think long and hard before making the decision to invite someone like Jesse into her home. After all, what did she really know about this boy? The answer was a simple one: She knew he needed their help.

Sitting in the hot tub that evening, Fiona and Michael talked about the commitment they would be making if Jesse agreed to stay with them. Many a difficult decision had been made in that hot tub. The darkness of the night, the warmth of the water and the soothing scent of eucalyptus always helped to put things into perspective. Every decision they had made so far had turned out to be the right one. Inviting Jesse into their home would be no exception.

Chapter 15

Friday was fast approaching and Jesse had not reacted to any of Connor's hints about coming to stay with him. There was only one thing left to do, Connor thought. He might as well come right out and suggest it. He'd go to the hospital tonight, right after his shift at the homeless shelter.

As Connor approached the shelter he saw a familiar figure sitting on the front steps. It was Jesse. But it was only Thursday, not Friday. What was he doing here a day early?

"Hey, Connor," said Jesse smugly. "They let me out for good behaviour."

"Are you sure you're okay, man? You look a little pale. How did you get here?"

"They sent me in a cab. Can you believe it? They gave all my meds to Mrs. Bradley."

"What's that on your lap?"

"It's my sketch pad. One of the guys here kept it safe for me."

"Could I see it?"

"Sure. It's just doodling. I like to draw cartoon characters."

Connor flipped open the spiral-bound pad and stared in disbelief at Jesse's drawings. He quickly unzipped his backpack and pulled out one of the posters he had drawn for the donor drive and handed it to Jesse. It was Jesse's turn to stare, his eyes big as saucers. The characters that Connor had drawn on his poster were eerily similar to Jesse's cartoon drawings.

"Cool!" they both said in unison.

"You know, I've been thinking," said Jesse. "The doctors at the hospital want me to come in for a bunch of tests and check-ups every couple of days for the next few weeks and since your house is so close I thought maybe I could crash at your place."

"Sure," said Connor with a slight shrug, trying hard to suppress a great big grin, "but I'd have to run it by my parents first. Let's go inside and use the phone at 'my' desk. I'm supposed to be on duty, you know."

Connor picked up his backpack and offered a hand to help Jesse up. The two of them walked into the shelter and headed straight for the reception desk. Connor called home and spoke to his mother nonchalantly, as if asking a parent if a homeless person could come and stay at your house was an everyday occurrence. His mother, on the other hand, couldn't suppress her delight. She wanted to ask how it all came about but she knew Jesse was right there with Connor and that he couldn't say much.

As soon as Connor hung up the phone, a group of Jesse's 'street family' approached them and wanted to know how Jesse was doing and whether he was back for good. Jesse explained his plan to stay at Connor's temporarily so that he could be close to the hospital. He made it sound like it was a decision of last resort and one that he had been reluctant to make.

Jesse then joined his friends as they headed back into the dining room for dinner. "I'll see you after dinner, Connor."

"Great. Then we'll head to my place."

Fiona arrived to find both boys ready and waiting at the main entrance to the shelter. Connor was carrying a drawstring bag, a satchel and an army-type duffle bag, along with his backpack. Mrs. Bradley, the shelter director, was standing next to them, holding a clear plastic food container full of pill vials.

Fiona parked the car, got out and went to meet both Jesse and Mrs. Bradley. "You must be Jesse," she said as she approached him with both her arms extended. "Do you mind if I give you a hug, since I feel I know you already?"

"I guess so," said Jesse tentatively, as he girded himself for one of Fiona's mama-bear hugs.

"You'd better get used to it, Jesse," said Connor with a smile. "She can't help herself. Mum, this is Mrs. Bradley. She's the director here. Mrs. Bradley, this is my mother, Fiona Hamilton."

"You've got quite a son, here Mrs. Hamilton," said Mrs. Bradley as they shook hands.

"Thank you for saying so, Mrs. Bradley, we think so too," said Fiona. "Connor, why don't you put Jesse's things into the car, while I have a chat with Mrs. Bradley?"

Connor and Jesse walked to the car while Mrs. Bradley and Fiona discussed the realities of Jesse's sickness combined with his lack of schooling, family, or financial support. Fiona assured the shelter director that she and her husband had discussed these very same issues and had made the decision to give Jesse all the support he needed to face the ordeal of either finding or not finding a bone marrow donor match. Mrs. Bradley was visibly relieved and turned her attention to the plastic food container she was holding. "These are Jesse's current meds," she said. "All the labels are self-explanatory and the most important thing is to remember they must be taken in a specific sequence; some first thing in the morning; some with food; some several times a day. I can't tell you what this means to all of us here, Mrs. Hamilton. Jesse is very special to us."

"I can see that, Mrs. Bradley," said Fiona, "and please call me Fiona. Why don't I give you weekly updates about Jesse? Do you have an email address I could use?"

"Updates would be wonderful, Fiona and please call me Louise," said Mrs. Bradley. "I'll post them on the bulletin board inside the dining room so that everyone can keep track of Jesse's progress."

With that, the two women hugged and said goodbye. Fiona walked over to the car to see that Connor was in the back seat. He'd given the front seat to Jesse. It may not have seemed like such a big gesture; however, with Connor chomping at the bit to begin his driver's ED classes, he relished every moment in the front seat gleaning what he could from his mother's driving capabilities. The way she seamlessly changed gear was like music to him; clutch in, gas off; clutch out, gas on – never any jerking or stalling or rolling back – revving the engine just right, simultaneously keeping her eye on the traffic, the tachometer and the speedometer. He couldn't wait to try it himself. But there he was, in the back seat, letting Jesse ride shotgun.

The ride home was surreal. Fiona tried to engage Jesse in conversation, but all she got were one-word answers. Even Connor's attempts to draw out more detailed responses from him were futile. Once home, they gathered in the kitchen where Michael was putting the final touches on their first dinner together with Jesse.

"Hi Michael, we've brought Jesse home," said Connor as Jesse stood beside him nervously cracking his knuckles and staring at the floor.

"Jesse, it's good to meet you at last," said Michael. "Connor has told us how proud he is to know you and so are we."

Jesse looked up to see Michael's warm smile and his hand proffered, not in anger, as had always been the case with Jesse's stepfather, but in friendship. When Jesse grasped Michael's hand, he felt as though he had taken hold of a lifeline that was pulling him to safety. "Thank you, sir," was all Jesse said.

Fiona's eyes brimmed with tears as she witnessed the hushed exchange of promise and understanding between her husband and Jesse. "Well," she said wiping away tears with the back of her hand, "let's get supper on the table."

It was decided that Jesse would take one of the guest bedrooms downstairs so that he could have his own bathroom and TV room. He could have used Frances' room for the next few weeks, since she was first staying at her mother's helping her recuperate from knee surgery and then flying off to Rome for her rugby tournament. However, Fiona felt Jesse was in need of some well-deserved privacy and quiet, both of which were sorely lacking in the hospital and at the shelter.

She'd give him a few days to settle in and then she would talk to him about getting back to school, either at home with a tutor or at the local high school down the road. For now, though, she was content to see him eating and sleeping well, taking his medications and letting his guard down long enough to allow a smile or two to lift his furrowed brow.

Chapter 16

A lot can happen in a month. Jesse responded well to home cooking and home schooling. Come to think of it, just <u>living</u> in a home was enough to breathe life into his disease-riddled body. He'd put on weight and had discovered the joys of owning a library card. Connor, much to Fiona's chagrin, wasn't much of a reader – of books, that is. Car and ski magazines he consumed with gusto but books in general left him cold. Jesse, on the other hand, was a voracious reader. Novels, biographies, even reference books, it didn't matter, Jesse devoured them all.

Jesse had settled in so well to the Hamilton-Kellaher household routine that when the phone rang one evening later that month, no one expected the caller would have news that would change their lives forever.

Fiona answered. The results from the bone marrow drive were in. They'd found not just a match but a perfect match for Jesse. It was Fiona herself.

She sat down hard on the bench next to the phone. "I beg your pardon? Would you repeat that again?" whispered Fiona into the receiver, not daring to believe what she'd heard.

It was true. She was a perfect match for Jesse.

"What was all that?" asked Michael, as he came into the kitchen to put on the kettle for their evening cup of tea.

"You're not going to believe this, but they found a donor match for Jesse," replied Fiona.

"That's terrific news. Do we know who it is?"

"Oh, yes, we know this person very well. It's me!"

Michael joined her on the bench, at a loss for words.

By this time, Jesse and Connor had come into the kitchen to see what all the commotion was about. Fiona rushed to Jesse, wrapped him in her arms and cried, "I knew it. I knew it. I knew it all along."

Jesse looked at Connor, then at Michael and said to Fiona, "What did you know? Who was that on the phone?"

Choked with emotion and unable to speak, Fiona gestured to Michael to give the boys the news that she was a perfect donor match for Jesse. "I told you I had a good feeling about the donor drive, Jesse," exclaimed Connor, giving him a high five.

"What do they mean by 'a perfect match'?" asked Jesse. "I thought a perfect match could only come from a family member?"

"Well," said Fiona, having recovered her voice, "the Canadian Blood Services wants me to come in for some further tests because they're asking the same question. But let's not look a gift horse in the mouth. Let's celebrate with a big bowl of butter-slathered popcorn and mocha hot chocolate."

The rest of the evening was spent looking up on the Internet all the steps involved with bone marrow donation; what the risks were; what the procedure entailed; and what the recovery time was like. As far as Fiona was concerned, it really didn't matter. She was prepared to do whatever it took.

As she looked over at Jesse, she could see that on the one hand he wanted to jump for joy, but on the other he didn't want to get his hopes up. "I know this is a lot for us all to absorb," Fiona said, "but let's take it one step at a time. Some steps might take us backwards and some may lead us to disappointments. But, look at how many steps forward we've taken so far."

Connor, Michael and Jesse all nodded in agreement.

Chapter 17

Before leaving for school the next morning, Connor called Lindsay to say he had exciting news and to meet him at the drop-off circle before chapel. Worcester Academy students were required to attend chapel every morning. It lasted about a half an hour and most students used it to catch up on reading assignments or sleep.

Connor watched the embassy limo pull into the circular drive. The burly bodyguard got out, opened the back door and out stepped Lindsay, her face bright and her uniform crisp and clean. Connor looked down at his wrinkled shirt and crooked house tie both of which were in serious need of spot remover. She ran over to him and said, "Well, what's the big news?"

"We got a call last night from the Canadian Blood Services and guess what?"

"What? Come on, Connor, I'm as jittery as a long-tailed cat in a room full of rocking chairs!"

"My Mum is a perfect donor match for Jesse! And what's that about your cat and a rocking chair? You sure have some colourful expressions."

"Never mind making fun of me and my accent Mr. 'eh' and 'oot and aboot'. This news about your Mum and Jesse is fantastic. Are they sure?"

"Well, she has to go in for further tests but the results are pretty clear."

"Maybe you should ask if you could make a school announcement. Everyone's dying to know."

They spread the word as they headed for chapel. After the service and on his way to his first class, Connor met Headmaster MacFarlane and told him the good news. It was decided that Connor would make an announcement at the end of the day.

Throughout the day, he let his mind reflect on the fact that his mother had been declared a 'perfect match'. Was it really true? If it was, what did it mean? Maybe they'd made a mistake. Surely, they wouldn't have called if they weren't one hundred percent certain. He couldn't shake the feeling of doubt creeping into his thoughts. He'd have to wait to really celebrate until the results were in from the further tests they were running on his mother's blood sample.

Luckily, he had Frances and Lindsay to keep him positive. They were both convinced that Fiona would be able to save Jesse's life. Their positive attitude lifted his spirits so that when he made his announcement at the end of the school day, he sounded so optimistic even he was convinced. Cheers roared through the halls once again and because the entire student body wanted to congratulate him as he made his way to Mac House, it took Connor forever to reach his locker.

The days were noticeably shorter and colder as Connor rode the bus home in the dark. The leaves along the bus route had turned their shimmering shades of red and gold. Winter was on the doorstep and he was looking forward to ski season. So much had happened since his Walkman had been stolen. He'd made such a fuss about it in the beginning but had to admit he didn't really miss it and hadn't felt the urge to get a new one.

Chapter 18

The following week, Fiona waited impatiently for the results from the further testing on her blood sample. When she asked what types of tests they were going to run, she was told that her DNA profile would be matched against Jesse's. She thought this was absurd and a complete waste of time. But, when the results came back and showed a familial link to Jesse, Fiona thought it was just plain crazy.

She called her brother, straight away. "Hi Tim, it's Fiona. I hope you're sitting down; otherwise you're going to fall down."

"Has something happened to Mum or Dad?"

"No, nothing like that. I've just heard from the Canadian Blood Services about the DNA analysis they ran on my blood sample against Jesse's. They say there's a familial match. That's crazy, right?"

"It sure sounds it. But it's almost impossible to make a mistake with the sophisticated DNA analysis that's performed

A Sheltered Life

these days. If you give me the name of the CBS contact, I'll give them a call, if you like."

"That would be great, Tim. I'd really appreciate it. But I don't want them to think I doubt their results and therefore brought in the heavy hitter from U of T for a second opinion."

"Don't worry. You know me, diplomacy is my middle name."

When Fiona broke the news to Connor and Jesse, they were both quiet to start with. Then the questions came fast and furious. Connor wanted to know exactly what was meant by 'familial' and how come only she was declared a 'perfect' match; Jesse wanted to know what would happen if they'd made a mistake and whether Fiona would still be considered at match for him even if it turned out the DNA analysis was wrong.

"These are all great questions," said Fiona. "We'll just have to wait to see what Uncle Tim finds out."

"How long is that going to take?" Connor groaned.

"He knows the head of the Canadian Blood Services very well, so I don't think it will take long at all," replied Fiona.

97

And she was right. But, instead of answering all their questions, the CBS had questions of their own. They asked Fiona to complete a myriad of forms about her family and then wanted blood samples from Fiona's Mum and Dad and from her brother, Tim, in order to run DNA profiles against Jesse's. The feeling was that if Fiona was related to Jesse, then so too was the rest of her family.

Again, they all waited. Fiona felt as though their lives were in limbo and every time the phone rang, she nearly jumped out of her skin. When the call finally came, it was from Tim. "Hold on to your hat, Fiona. You thought you were surprised to hear you were related to Jesse. Wait 'til you hear this. The only one of us who is NOT related to him is our mother!"

"You've got to be kidding."

"I'm not. I ran the tests myself and I've gone over the results with a fine-toothed comb."

"Let me get this straight. You and I are related; Connor and Dad are related; but Mum is not."

"That's exactly right. You see, you are the daughter of a rocket scientist!"

"This is no time for jokes, Tim. What does it all mean?"

"At this point, your guess is as good as mine. Who's going to tell Mum and Dad?"

"I think we should tell them together. Obviously, there are some blanks here that only they can fill in."

"I was thinking the same thing. Why don't I fly up this weekend and lay it all out so that it's easy for us to see what's missing?"

"That would be great. Call me when you're on the ground and I'll come and pick you up," said Fiona.

"Was that Tim on the phone?" asked Michael as he came into the bedroom where Fiona was sitting on her favourite chaise longue with the handset still in her hand. "You look a little dazed. Was the news that shocking?"

She patted the seat beside her and Michael sat down. She then told him what Tim had discovered through the DNA analysis. Once she'd finished, Tim suggested they give the news to Connor and Jesse.

They were downstairs playing Super Mario when Fiona called them to come up to the kitchen. "I've just been speaking with Uncle Tim," said Fiona as the boys sat with them at the table. "He's given us the most incredible news. He says that he, Connor, Grandad and I are all related somehow to Jesse and that Gran is the only one of us who is not."

She let Connor and Jesse absorb what they'd just heard and then added that Uncle Tim was coming to Ottawa on the weekend to explain his findings to all of them, including Connor's Gran and Grandad.

"Does this mean you guys are my family?" asked Jesse.

"I don't know how or why just yet, Jesse," said Fiona, "but yes it does and yes we are!"

Jesse got up, went to Fiona and put his arms around her shoulders as his shook with emotion. This was the first time he had shown any outward feeling toward her and she responded by patting his back and soothing him as he sobbed like a child. Connor and Michael joined in the group hug. Needless to say, there wasn't a dry eye in the house.

Chapter 19

On Friday when Tim called to say he'd landed, Fiona headed to the airport to pick him up. He waved to her as she pulled up to the curb. As usual, he had only two bags – a carry-on with wheels and a leather satchel. He never had checked luggage, if he could help it, because he never wanted to waste time waiting at the baggage carousel. His signature brown, suede fedora was strategically tipped in such a way as to give him an air of mystery and to protect him from the prying eyes of autograph seekers.

Here he was, a world-renowned haematologist and best-selling medical mystery writer and all Fiona could see was a boy who teased her mercilessly. On family outings with them in the back seat of the car, Tim would take advantage of any of his sister's visible bruises by telling her that he was a doctor and wanted to make sure the bruises weren't serious ones. He would start to press his finger on the bruise and tell her he would stop when it hurt. Of course he would then press harder eliciting a squeal and earning them a swift reprimand (verbal and physical) from the front seat.

"Hello my darling sister," he said as he opened the car door, put his bags on the back seat and sat next to her.

"Hey there brother of mine," said Fiona, as she leaned over to give him a kiss on the cheek. "Any deranged Tim Hamilton fans on the flight?"

"None at all. I only had to sign one autograph and that was for the flight attendant."

"So, I guess we're in for an interesting time this weekend. What's your current theory?"

"I honestly don't have one. I doubt whether I could even hatch one to use in my next book! It's obvious, though, that Dad holds the key."

"It'll be interesting to see their reaction. I've kept them up to speed on Jesse's progress and they came to the donor drive to cheer us on. They know I've been declared a perfect match for Jesse and they're just as puzzled as the rest of us."

"Well, that must mean they're not aware of any skeletons in the closet."

"I guess we'll just have to make some rattling noises, then."

They arrived home to find all the lights on, music blaring and a pizza delivery man pounding on the back door. Fiona paid for the pizzas and she and Tim ventured into the house. Michael was topping up the hot tub and was oblivious to the cacophony of sound swirling around him. He gave quite a start when Fiona tapped him on the shoulder. He turned around to see his favourite brother-in-law mouthing the words 'how can you stand all this noise?'

"Come on, Tim," said Michael, as they hugged each other warmly, "you've got teenagers; you know what it's like. Connor wanted to have 'a couple' of friends over to meet Jesse."

"I've put the pizza on the counter but maybe I'll take it downstairs along with the music," said Fiona.

She headed to the kitchen just as Connor was coming in from the front hall. "Hi Mum, is Uncle Tim here?" he asked.

"He's out on the veranda. Go and say hi and then please take your pizza and your music downstairs so we can have a conversation that doesn't strain our vocal chords."

"Okay and thanks for letting me have some friends over to meet Jesse."

"That's what this house is for, but please keep an eye on Jesse. Don't let him get too tired."

"I won't. Hey, do you think I should offer Lindsay's chauffeur and bodyguard some pizza? They're just sitting outside in the car."

"There's no harm in asking. Maybe you should bring Lindsay with you so they won't think you've laced it with arsenic or something," said Fiona laughing.

She went to the fridge, got three beers and took them out to Tim and Michael. The three of them sat in the overstuffed wicker chairs and took long draughts of their lagers. Miraculously, the music stopped and was replaced by soothing silence.

"That's better," said Fiona. "Is there anything you need us to do before Mum and Dad come over tomorrow?"

"As long as we all have a comfortable chair and some good light, I think we should be fine," replied Tim. "I've explained the Human Leukocyte Antigen or HLA match between you and Jesse using a simple diagram and I'll do my best to answer any questions as simply as I can. As for the DNA match, well, that's a whole different ball game."

"That's for sure," said Fiona. "We'll just have to ask the right questions. The first question is where do we start?"

Chapter 20

The next morning, at precisely ten o'clock, in through the back door came Fiona's father, 82-year-old James Hamilton. Never one to be late or to knock and wait to be invited in, Mr. Hamilton greeted everyone with his customary, "What's going on here, then?" His Scottish lilt was still perceptible even though he'd lived in Canada for almost fifty years. As always, Ann Hamilton was not far behind.

The fact that her parents lived right across the street in her childhood home was both a blessing and a curse. On the one hand, she loved the fact that her children could just run over to see their grandparents at a moment's notice; on the other, she could see that their dependence on her was growing. Fiona and Michael had bought their house knowing full well that the day would come when the burden of care for her parents would become more than she could handle. For the time being, though, they relished the time they were able to spend with these two energetic octogenarians.

Fiona had her father's coffee already poured and sitting on the table along with this week's cryptic crossword clipped from the Saturday paper. She and her father had a standing date every Saturday morning. They'd have a coffee, a cookie and start (and usually complete) the weekly mind bender. It was said the mind had to work in a certain kind of way – on many levels at once - in order to grasp the hidden meanings within the clues and anagrams to solve cryptic crosswords. Her father was a genius at it and had taught his daughter well from a very early age. James Hamilton was a genius, period. Fiona often joked that she knew things or could do things because she was the 'daughter of a rocket scientist'. Well, it was true. Her father had been a brilliant chemical engineer and propellants expert with the Department of National Defence for 35 years.

"I'm not sure we'll have time today to get started on the crossword, Dad," said Fiona. "Tim wants to explain to us why I'm a perfect bone marrow match for Jesse. We're just waiting for the boys to join us."

With that, Connor and Jesse sluggishly made their appearance in the kitchen and sat down next to Connor's grandparents at the table.

"Hi Gran, hi Grandad," said Connor sleepily.

"Good morning Mr. and Mrs. Hamilton," said Jesse.

"Good morning boys," said Ann. "I see your Uncle Tim is about to give us one of his famous medical lectures. Jesse, you should know that whatever we find out today, you will still have our full support." Ann would soon find these last words difficult to keep.

"Good," said Tim, "we're all here. This shouldn't take too long to explain and please, if you have any questions along the way, just ask them."

He produced a series of colourful charts and graphs and took his family through a rudimentary explanation of what it meant to be a perfect bone marrow match. He started by explaining that Human Leukocyte Antigens (HLA) are located on the outside of white blood cells (leukocytes) and on most other cells in the body; an Antigen is a substance, usually a molecule, that triggers the immune system to respond to it. He told them that for a bone marrow transplant, the HLA need to be virtually identical – or perfect – in the donor and the recipient. Otherwise, the recipient will reject the new marrow or the donor marrow will multiply and attack the recipient's tissues.

In Fiona's and Jesse's case, Tim explained that not only did his sister have a 7/8 HLA match, which was quite a surprise, she also had an HLA-C match that was particularly rare. It was for this reason that the DNA analysis was requested – the same reason that had brought them all together that day.

"Now we get to the tricky part," said Tim. "We have to figure out why all of our DNA profiles, except for Mum's, show a familial match."

Fiona looked around the table to see heads shaking and shoulders shrugging. "Let's start with what we do know and maybe that will help us figure out what we don't know," she said. Everyone nodded in agreement.

She began by stating the facts: Jesse Brown was born in Ottawa 16 years ago. His mother's name was Patricia. According to Jesse, she had no family. Jesse and his mother moved to Toronto when Jesse was a two-year-old. According to Jesse, his mother was in her early forties when she died. Therefore, she would have been born in the early 1960s.

Fiona noticed her mother frown and then start to say something, only to be interrupted by her father.

"This is getting us nowhere," said Mr. Hamilton. "Come and get me when you've figured it out." He stood up and started for the door.

"Sit down, James, for Heaven's sake!" said Mrs. Hamilton. "I think I can shed some light here." She hesitated and then said, "I think Jesse might be Patsy's son."

"Patsy? Our sister, Patsy?" asked Fiona incredulously. Her mother nodded. "Why would you think that?"

Patsy had been adopted by the Hamilton's in 1960, when she was 4 years old. At the time, the family lived just east of Calgary, Alberta in a town called Ralston.

"All the dates match," said Mrs. Hamilton. "We know that Patsy ran away from home when she was 16. But I knew she had stayed in Ottawa because on one of my volunteer days at the Children's Aid, a two-month-old baby came in to be evaluated for placement in foster care. The mother's name was Patricia Hamilton and the baby's name was Jesse James Hamilton. Her baby was placed with a wonderful family and just before he turned two they asked Patsy if they could adopt him. After one of her scheduled outings with Jesse, she failed to return him to the family. Now it looks as though she ran away to Toronto."

There was silence around the table as they all tried to come to terms with what Ann Hamilton had just told them. "Jesse, have you got a picture of your mother?" asked Fiona.

"Not a very good one."

"Would you go and get it for us, please?"

"Sure, it's in my duffle bag," said Jesse as he hurried down the hall to the back staircase. He returned carrying what looked like a bus pass holder and handed it to Fiona. She took it, carefully opened it and stared at the worn and faded photograph. She said nothing as she passed it to her mother.

"Well, would someone please say something?" said Connor, his voice rising.

The photo came full circle around the table. "That's Patsy," said Fiona finally. "Her hair is darker and she's thinner, but that's definitely her."

Jesse hadn't moved. He was still standing in front of Fiona. She stood up and put her arm around him. "That's one mystery solved," she said. "Now let's see if we can figure out the blood connection."

"Wait a minute," said Connor. "I'm still trying to unravel the first mystery in my mind. Let me get this straight. Jesse's mother was your and Uncle Tim's adopted sister and Gran, you met Jesse when he was just a little baby and didn't tell anyone about it. Then, Jesse's mother runs away with him and nobody tries to find out where they went or what happened to them?"

"When you put it like that, Connor, it does sound odd," said his grandmother. "But at the time, I felt that Jesse would be well looked after by the foster family and that Patsy would come to realise that she could still play an important role in Jesse's life even after the foster family had adopted him. As for not saying anything when Jesse first came into the Children's Aid, I thought it would be upsetting to Fiona. In hindsight, I realise I made a tragic mistake and for that I'm truly sorry." She reached into her pocket and pulled out a handkerchief to wipe away her tears. "When Patsy didn't return with Jesse, our hands were tied at the Children's Aid. She had every right to take him since she had placed him in foster care voluntarily."

"It's okay, Mum, we all do things that we think are best for our family," said Fiona, as she reached over and patted her mother's hand. "On the bright side, we've found our long-lost nephew, cousin and grandson. What could be better than that?" She looked over at Jesse who was shaking his head.

"When I was in Grade 6, we had to draw our family tree," Jesse said solemnly. "I asked my mother to help me and she said, 'There's just the two of us, Jesse James'. When I asked her why, she just said she'd caused her family so much pain that they'd never want to speak to me about my project. You should have seen some of the family trees that the other kids handed in. Mine was just pathetic."

"Let's see if we can add a few more branches to that tree, Jesse," said Tim. "Dad, you are the main link in this chain. Is there anything you can remember that would help us unravel this unseemly family connection?"

James, who had remained silent to this point, was deep in thought as Ann, still on the verge of tears, nodded to her husband silently giving him permission to speak.

He began by telling them that when Fiona was a year old, he and Ann decided to separate. He moved from their home in Ralston, Alberta to Calgary and met a woman with whom he'd had a very brief affair. He hadn't thought of or heard from the woman since. The following year he and Ann reconciled and he moved back to Ralston. He told his wife about the affair; they sought counselling and then decided they wanted another child. As Ann had undergone a hysterectomy shortly after Fiona's birth, they decided to adopt.

It took almost three years before all the screening, interviews and paperwork were completed. In the 1960s in Alberta, a father could not be more than 40 years older than the adopted child and as James was 44 that year, he and Ann decided to open their home to a 4-year-old girl, named Patricia – Patsy for short. The Hamiltons then had a year to decide whether or not to keep Patsy – a decision they agonized over when the time came.

Fiona and Tim gaped at each other and then at their parents. It had just dawned on them that Patsy, their adopted sister from the orphanage in Calgary, was actually related to them. Incredibly, Patsy was James Hamilton's daughter and Fiona's and Tim's half-sister.

"Good gracious!" said Ann Hamilton. "That explains why I'm the only one without the DNA match."

"All those years and none of us had any idea," said James, shaking his head.

"Wait a minute. Sorry to keep asking for clarification but does this mean that your adopted sister, Patsy, was really your sister?" asked Connor.

"That seems to be the case," said Fiona as she looked over at Jesse who was now nodding his head and smiling. "Tell us what you're smiling at, Jesse."

"Remember, Connor, when you asked where my nickname, Switcher, came from and I told you it's because I switch hands to play hockey – just like you?" asked Jesse.

"Yeah," said Connor grinning, "and then we saw that our cartoon drawings were almost identical."

"Well I guess it's because it's in our genes!" exclaimed Jesse.

Chapter 21

Fiona vividly remembered, almost at age six, travelling by car from Ralston to Calgary to pick up her 'new' sister, Patsy, from the orphanage. At the time, she didn't understand the meaning of the word 'orphanage' but recalled being ushered into a large room with a row of chairs that faced a glass wall – sort of like a mirror but more like a tinted window. There were very few lights on in the room with the chairs but the room on the other side of the window was full of light and teaming with children. She sat down next to her mother who leaned over and said, "Do you see that little girl in the green and yellow dress, sitting on the stool? That's your new sister, Patsy."

"How old is she?" asked Fiona.

"She's four – about two years younger than you."

"Where are her parents?"

"She has no parents. That's why she lives here at the orphanage."

"Is that why she's coming to live with us?"

"Yes, it is Fiona. We thought you'd be a perfect sister for her."

Fiona nodded and noticed that Patsy wasn't playing with the other children; that she looked sad and lonely. Fiona's eyes never left Patsy's face as her parents and an older woman with grey hair pulled back into a bun spoke in hushed tones and shuffled through a seemingly endless stack of paper.

Fiona felt odd, like she was spying on this little girl who was to be her new sister. Not once did Patsy look up or over at her. Even when Fiona waved, Patsy seemed not to notice. But her mother did and quickly explained to her that they were looking at Patsy through a two-way mirror; they could see her but she couldn't see them.

Fiona watched as a tall woman in a red-and-white flowered dress came over to Patsy and took her hand. Patsy stood up, picked up what Fiona had thought was a stool and walked out of the room. A few moments later, there was a knock at the door and Fiona instinctively went over and opened it. There stood her new sister, carrying a brown and red overnight case and looking down at the floor.

"Hi, I'm Fiona. You must be my new sister Patsy," said Fiona.

Patsy remained silent, her eyes fixed on her shoes. Fiona noticed that Patsy was the same height as she was, even though Fiona was older. She also noticed that Patsy's cheek was swollen and there was crusted blood on her lip.

Ann approached Patsy and patted her on the back. "Cat got your tongue, Patsy?" she asked.

The woman in the red-and-white flowered dress explained to them that Patsy had just come back from the dentist where she'd had a tooth pulled. "Her cheek is a little swollen and she'll need to take some painkillers for the rest of the day," she said. "I wouldn't expect her to be very chatty."

Fiona's father was still sitting on his chair staring blankly at the newest member of his family. "Come on, James," said Ann taking Patsy's hand, "make yourself useful and carry Patsy's suitcase."

The four of them made their way outside to the car. As James opened the trunk of their 1959 Chevrolet Biscayne to stow Patsy's suitcase, a wail that quickly turned into a high-pitched scream escaped from her throat. Frightened, Fiona covered her ears and hid behind her mother. Still screaming at the top of her lungs, Patsy let go of Ann's hand and reached desperately for her precious suitcase.

"It's her suitcase, James," said Ann, her voice raised to be heard over Patsy's. "She wants to have it with her."

"Well, she'd better get out of the habit of screeching like that to get her own way," shouted James as he slammed the trunk and thrust the case to Patsy who immediately stopped screaming.

Patsy didn't say a word on the hour-long drive home from Calgary to Ralston, despite Fiona's attempts to engage her in conversation. Fiona tried to entice her with colouring books and crayons and with her favourite game – "Eye Spy", but to no avail.

Once home, Fiona took Patsy upstairs to show her their room. There were bunk beds along the left wall and a red metal crib straight ahead, underneath the window.

"This is my bed, and Mum says that one is yours," said Fiona, sitting on the bottom bunk and pointing toward the crib.

That night, Fiona was startled awake by Patsy's screaming. She looked over to see her sister kneeling in the crib, her hands wrapped around the metal bars rattling them like she was trying to escape from a prison cell. Her mother ran into the room and turned on the overhead light, demanding to know what all the fuss was about. There seemed to be little she could do to calm Patsy down and then as quickly as it started, the noise stopped and Patsy fell asleep.

"She must have had a bad dream. She'll be alright now." said Ann, as she turned out the light and headed back to her room.

In the morning, Ann lifted Patsy out of the crib and led her quickly to the bathroom. Fiona was glad she didn't have to rely on her mother to get her out of bed and take her to the bathroom. As she was getting dressed, Fiona glanced at Patsy's open suitcase. It was small, light brown and rectangular in shape with a red top and clear handle. It also had a large, spring-loaded clasp on the front. Fiona's mother had a similar one that she packed her toiletries in when they went on holiday. Inside Patsy's, she could see a hairbrush, a pair of shorts, two T-shirts, a couple of pairs of well-worn underpants, a blue scarf and a stick of chewing gum.

Fiona was particularly drawn to the gum because it wasn't allowed in the Hamilton household – 'only common people chew the wretched stuff' to quote her father. It was then that she realized that the contents of this tattered overnight case represented all of her sister's belongings. Nothing else had come with them in the car and Fiona hadn't heard that anything was being sent later. Imagine being able to pack your whole life into one little suitcase, she thought.

The first week that Fiona spent with her new sister was full of adventure. Even though Patsy didn't say much, she was an eager participant in Fiona's daily routines. One of the most memorable was when Fiona asked her mother whether she could bring Patsy for 'Show and Tell' to her Grade One class. Mrs. Hamilton agreed without a second thought and the two of them set off on their three-block journey to school. After arriving at Mrs. Whitney's class, Fiona proudly introduced Patsy to her teacher as her new sister.

Mrs. Whitney's reaction was not quite what Fiona had expected. Instead of smiling and asking Patsy to join them in their morning story circle, as she normally did when they had special visitors, Mrs. Whitney took both their hands and led them down the hall to Principal Thain's office. Fiona was frightened. She'd never been to the Principal's office before; although, she'd heard stories from her brother, Tim, about bad children being sent there to 'get the strap'.

"Fiona, I want you to repeat to Principal Thain what you told me about this young girl you brought with you to school today," said Mrs. Whitney rather sternly.

"I, I said that I had brought my new sister Patsy for 'Show and Tell'," said Fiona nervously.

Mr. Thain's eyebrows rose sharply. "Exactly my reaction," said Mrs. Whitney. "I think you should call Ann Hamilton straight away in case this young girl has been reported missing."

Mr. Thain pondered Mrs. Whitney's request. After all, this was his boss' wife they were thinking about calling out of the blue to ask whether her daughter had perhaps kidnapped a young girl on her way to school. James Hamilton was not just his boss but everyone's boss in the village of Ralston and the adjoining Canadian Forces Base Suffield, where the Defence Research Board had established an experimental station to study rocket propellants and to research biological and chemical warfare applications. He'd have to choose his words very carefully, since James Hamilton was the Base's current Chief Superintendent.

Reluctantly, he picked up the telephone receiver and asked his secretary to place a call to Ann Hamilton. "Good morning Ann. It's Reg Thain," said the principal.

"Good morning, Reg. Is this a social call?"

"Yes and no. First, I wanted to thank you for inviting Lillian and me for dinner to meet Prime Minister Diefenbaker next week. We'd love to come. The second reason for my call is to let you know that a young girl has accompanied Fiona to school today. Fiona has introduced her as her new sister and I wasn't aware that..."

"She's absolutely right, Reg!" interrupted Mrs. Hamilton. "Perhaps I should have called to let you know but I didn't think it would create such a stir. Is she causing any trouble?"

"No trouble at all. She's more than welcome to spend the day with Fiona. Lillian and I are looking forward to seeing you next week, Ann. Goodbye." Relieved the call was over, Mr. Thain hung up the telephone, opened the top drawer of his desk, took out two peppermints and handed them to Fiona and Patsy.

Fiona reached for hers but Patsy hung back. "It's okay, Patsy. It's a peppermint candy," said Fiona. Patsy looked at Fiona, smiled and held out her hand. For the first time since Patsy's arrival, Fiona thought she and her sister would get along just fine – and they did, for the most part.

Right from the start, Ann Hamilton treated Fiona and Patsy like twins, even though Patsy was almost two years younger than Fiona and not fair-skinned with freckles like her sister. Their mother dressed them in the same clothes – in different colours; gave them the same gifts – in different colours. She even gave them the same haircuts. But oddly enough, everyone remarked – even joked – that while Fiona and Tim were the spitting image of their mother, Patsy took after her adopted father. She had the same long nose as he did and shared his darker skin tone.

The first year of Patsy's life with the Hamiltons proved to be a difficult one. She was a troubled child who screamed nightly, stole daily and lied incessantly. It was understandable, though, since by the time she was four, she had been adopted by two families, prior to Fiona's. The reason given for Patsy's return to the orphanage on both occasions was that the families hadn't bonded with her. Not much was known about her background other than her mother was an alcoholic and declared unfit when Patsy was three. She had died suddenly leaving Patsy with no family. The identity and whereabouts of her father were unknown.

Four years after Patsy's arrival, Fiona and her family moved to Ottawa. Unfortunately, her sister's life continued to be fraught with lies and deceit, expanding into drugs and ultimately total alienation from the family. At the age of 16, Patsy contracted hepatitis from mainlining speed using a dirty syringe and spent two weeks in hospital. This revelation came as a complete shock to her parents. Fiona, on the other hand, had known for some time that her sister had been popping pills of all shapes and colours. Patsy had even proudly showed Fiona the needle marks between her toes where she'd been injecting goodness knows what. Laughing uncontrollably about how gullible their parents were, Patsy would boast to Fiona about her antics at school and about her extracurricular activities often involving theft and vandalism.

It never occurred to Fiona to 'rat' on her sister. Instead, she tried to convince her to stay away from her so-called friends – some of whom were much older. This, too, was met with fits of laughter from Patsy.

During her stay in hospital, the only member of the family to visit Patsy was her father. By then, she had taken to calling them Mr. and Mrs. Hamilton as she no longer considered them her parents. Ann had stopped calling Patsy by her name and instead referred to her as 'the lodger'. At the dinner table, after his visit to Patsy, James recounted that the only reason he'd gone to the hospital that day was to strike a deal with her. He told her would set her up in her own apartment and pay all her expenses, since she would not be welcome at home for the time being. The only things he asked in return were that she stay away from drugs and that she finish high school. Her response to him consisted of an obscene hand gesture and a string of profanities that spewed from her mouth. Following her father's revelation, Fiona remained silent, unlike her mother.

Annoyed that her husband had ignored her expressed desire to cut all ties with Patsy, Ann chided, "Well, what did you think she'd do James? Apologize and take you up on your ridiculous offer? I can't believe you tried to bribe her like that."

"Surely, you can appreciate the delicate situation I'm in, Ann. She threatened to make our lives a living hell – more than the hell we're in now. My level of security clearance at the office will not tolerate any type of threat – particularly from a close family member. Who knows what she's capable of." replied James. "I did what I thought was best for the family."

"It sounds more like blackmail to me," said Ann tartly.

In the weeks that followed, Fiona learned that her sister had made calls to many of their parents' well-heeled friends pretending to be Fiona, asking for money and begging them not to tell her parents. Patsy was also arrested for alleged prostitution and drug possession.

Other than a court-scheduled visit to the house to pick up some of her things, Fiona never saw her sister again – ever. Fiona recalled that her sister had taken with her only things their father had given to her: a book on dogs, a small wooden bowl that he had turned on his lathe and a brush and comb set that had belonged to his mother - Granny Hamilton. At age 16, Patsy was an emancipated minor and therefore the Hamiltons were not legally required to make any effort to find her – and they didn't. Instead, they took all the steps necessary to disown her.

Chapter 21

Even though thinking of her sister brought back painful memories, Fiona realized that it had been worth all the hurt, disappointment, anger and frustration since she was now in a position to make some good come from it. For Jesse's sake, she would concentrate on the good times she'd had with her sister so that she could share them with Jesse. She also concentrated on the looming timetable for Jesse's bone marrow transplant.

It was now early November and the transplant was scheduled for the first week of December. During his last visit, Tim had described what Fiona and Jesse could expect in terms of the procedure and recovery time. He made it very clear that it would not be a walk in the park for either of them. He also explained how Jesse's diseased marrow would be replaced with healthy cells from Fiona. He told them that to prepare for the transplant Jesse would be given high doses of radiation and/or chemotherapy to destroy the diseased marrow. At that point, stripped of the ability to manufacture life-giving blood cells, Jesse would be extremely vulnerable to infection. He wouldn't survive unless Fiona were to proceed with the donation. Once collected from Fiona, the healthy stem cells would be given intravenously to Jesse as soon as possible.

Fiona would have to undergo a somewhat painful and invasive procedure. Bone marrow is usually harvested near the hips, in the middle of the lower back. Fiona would be given a local anaesthetic at the spot where a small finger drill would enter. Since there is no way to freeze the bone itself, she would feel some discomfort as a hole was drilled into the bone so that the marrow could be extracted. She was glad to hear that the whole procedure wouldn't take more than a few minutes and that she would feel only slight tenderness afterward but nothing requiring heavy medication.

In the weeks leading up to Jesse's bone marrow transplant, the family grew closer. Connor and Jesse were inseparable. Jesse was eager to show Connor how well he was doing with his studies and Connor, in turn, dedicated more time to homework and less to TV and video games. It looked as though a competition was brewing to see who could get the better marks. Fiona sensed there might be more to Jesse's push to learn as much as he could before he began his treatments. She felt he wanted to fill his mind with as much information as it could hold so that if the chemotherapy were to destroy more than just his bone marrow, he'd still have some knowledge left.

Fiona also noticed that the only one who didn't warm to Jesse was her mother. She couldn't tell whether her mother was upset because Patsy was her father's illegitimate child or whether her mother felt guilty about abandoning Patsy; not giving her another chance. Fiona couldn't imagine giving up on a son or daughter – adopted or not. She knew her mother lacked patience and was quick to pass judgement. But she also knew that, for Ann Hamilton and her family, it just wouldn't have been acceptable to talk or seek help about drugs – let alone admit you had a child with a drug problem. Had Patsy suffered from fetal alcohol syndrome – a disease that involves growth, mental, and physical problems that may occur in a baby when a mother drinks alcohol during pregnancy? Was she afflicted with a mental illness such as obsessive compulsive disorder? Had she been bi-polar? To Fiona's knowledge, none of these questions had ever been asked or, more importantly, answered.

Fiona's father, on the other hand, grew fonder of Jesse every day. It was difficult for Fiona to use the word 'love' when describing her father's feelings toward anyone. But with Jesse he was much more demonstrative, giving him more hugs than she could ever remember receiving and offering him endless words of encouragement. It was as though he was trying to make up for lost time.

Connor, too, enjoyed listening to his grandfather as he told the two of them about all the one-of-kind contraptions he built for his children. There was the tandem bicycle fashioned from two, broken bikes he'd found in the neighbour's trash. One blue and one red, the two orphaned bikes were welded together and joined by one long chain with two sets of pedals and handlebars. Fiona and Patsy used that tandem as a regular taxi service, picking up and dropping off their friends from all over the neighbourhood. They became quite adept at tire, brake and chain repair, as malfunctions and break-downs were frequent. That was the thing about everything their father made; patience, cunning and good luck all played major roles in the success and longevity of their use.

There was also the gas-powered go-kart constructed using an old washing machine motor, some corrugated metal, baby carriage wheels and radio knobs (for the throttle and choke). However, it had no brakes. Fiona, Tim and Patsy had to learn very quickly to finesse the throttle in order to make quick turns, avoid collisions and glide smoothly to a stop – without revving or choking the engine.

"It couldn't have gone very fast, Grandad," said Connor.

"Quite the contrary, Connor, it had lots of pep!" replied James. "And your mother was the best driver. She was a natural."

"What about my mother?" asked Jesse.

"Your mother was more cautious," said James. "But she loved to ride shotgun with Fiona."

"How old were they?" asked Jesse.

"Hmm, let me think. We were still on the prairie when I built the first one, so the two girls must have been 7 and 9 at the time. They drove it on the runways at the Suffield airbase so there was lots of room to manoeuvre. Then, I built another one when we moved to Ottawa and they used the street as their racetrack. The turn-around point was the Turner's circular driveway on the far corner."

The story Connor liked the best was the one about the kayak that Grandad had built for Unlce Tim. Still in use at their cottage, Connor was almost too big for it now, but it was the first boat he ever operated solo and what a thrill that had been. Long, sleek and narrow, it rode effortlessly in the water and was propelled with a two-headed paddle that took some practice to get right.

When the boys asked why he built the kayak, James told them it was his love of the Arctic that had led to his fascination with this one-man watercraft. He marvelled at its history, its versatility and the fact that it was absolutely essential to the survival of the Inuit (Eskimos as they were called when James worked in the Arctic).

He was introduced to Canada's north when the family was posted to the Defence Research Northern Laboratory, in Fort Churchill, Manitoba shortly before Fiona was born. He was captivated by the tundra, the Aurora Borealis, the polar bears and the Inuit. Fiona's birth at Fort Churchill's military hospital was somewhat of a rarity. James joked with the boys that he knew they'd brought home the right baby since Fiona was the only pink face in a sea of bright red ones peaking out of their bassinettes in the hospital nursery.

On the day she was born, her father bundled up his then three-year-old son Tim in his parka, mukluks and mittens, sat him on the toboggan and began pulling him along the snow-covered path to the hospital. About half way there, James glanced back at the toboggan only to see that it was empty! Somewhere along the way, Tim had been blown off by the bitter winter wind. James knew he'd get a pretty frosty reception from his wife if he were to arrive at the hospital to meet his new daughter having just lost his son. He retraced his steps and found Tim lodged in a snow bank, unable to move because of the thickness of his outerwear.

Since children were not permitted in the maternity ward of the hospital, Tim wouldn't be allowed in to visit his mother and baby sister. Rocket scientist that he was, this did not deter James. He trudged alongside the one-storey building until he found his wife's room. Since the snow was so high, he had no trouble knocking on the window to attract her attention. She arrived at the window with baby Fiona in her arms, as her husband was lifting Tim onto his shoulders. Ann just managed to smile and wave when all of a sudden her husband disappeared from view. She looked down to see him chest-deep in the snow still holding Tim on his shoulders! Heat from the building had weakened the snow against the wall and James had sunk down to his chest. A quick call was made to the MPs on the base and the two Hamilton men were extricated without injury – at least no physical ones!

"Churchill is known as the 'Polar Bear Capital of the World', said James.

"I knew that," said Connor. "It's because they migrate right through the centre of town on their way to and from hunting harp seals in Hudson's Bay."

"That's right, Connor. You must have been paying attention in geography class. What you might not know, is that during the time of their migration, in the spring and fall, there is an unwritten rule in Churchill that doors are to be left unlocked. Then, if you are confronted by a polar bear, you are to walk backwards slowly up to the nearest house, open the door and back yourself in. It's unfortunate that Fort Churchill was completely bulldozed many years ago. The only thing left is the vehicle maintenance garage that's now used as the polar bear jail."

"As soon as Churchill was mentioned, I told my class that my Mum was born just down the road in Fort Churchill. After that, I found it easy to remember everything about the polar bears and their habitat. We learned that they're attracted to the open-air dump nearby and can become aggressive and a danger to the public. They're drugged, tagged and then taken to the polar bear jail. Is it true that the bears are only allowed to return a couple of times or else they're killed?"

"It usually doesn't come to that Connor. The bears are air-lifted to remote areas and their time in jail discourages them from returning."

Even though the family was posted to Ralston, Alberta shortly after Fiona was born, James never lost his love and fascination for the North.

Chapter 22

The day finally came when Jesse entered the Children's hospital to begin his month-long, intensive chemotherapy treatments. He would remain in an isolation unit for the duration of the treatments, since destroying his bone marrow would also destroy his ability to fight infection.

Fiona visited Jesse daily, donning the mandatory, sickly green hospital gown, gloves and mask before entering his room. Each day she brought photographs she'd found by scouring her parents' basement.

Her favourite one was of Patsy, herself and their black standard poodle Caesar. How Patsy loved that dog. He followed the girls everywhere but slept at the end of Fiona's bed since hers was the bottom bunk. Tim couldn't get Caesar to sleep in his room no matter how hard he tried. He even tied Caesar to his bedpost one night but had to let him go when the constant whimpering became too much to bear. One Sunday, at church where all three children sang in the choir, they stared in amazement as Caesar appeared at the front doors and proudly trotted up the aisle to the altar, his dog tags jingling. Ann, who was both organist and choir mistress, calmly snapped her fingers twice from her organ bench and Caesar obediently walked to her side and lay down for the duration of the service.

Other photos captured Fiona and her sister on family camping trips. James always took his summer holidays the first two weeks of July, without fail. They camped across Canada from the Okanagan Valley to the Badlands to Prince Edward Island. It was at Rustico Beach on Prince Edward Island where Patsy accidentally hit Fiona full force in the head with a golf club. That particular snapshot showed Fiona lying on her side on a picnic table with Patsy sitting glumly on the bench while their mother stood and poured peroxide into the gaping wound on the side of Fiona's head. For weeks, she sported a bleached-blond patch of hair the size of a hockey puck to remind her of the mishap.

To this day, Fiona disliked camping. Wet tents, damp sleeping bags, leaking air mattresses and bugs in the pancake batter were all things she would rather live without. When Michael was asked once whether Fiona liked to sleep under the stars he replied, "yes, five stars!"

There were other photos of school trips, special holidays and celebrations. Fiona was surprised she found as many as she did, since there weren't any of Patsy past the age of 14 – about the time she began to hang around with the 'bad lot' as her parents referred to the circle of friends she had adopted. Jesse was mesmerized by the photographs. He poured over them again and again and asked a myriad of questions. What's she doing here? Why are you both wearing the same clothes? Who's that with her? What's she holding? Why is she pulling you in a wagon? Why isn't she smiling? As long-held memories floated to the surface, Fiona answered each question as best she could.

She told him about the time she was hit by a car, at the age of ten, on her way home from ballet class one evening in February. She had just stepped off the bus and had begun to cross the street just as the bus pulled away from the stop. It was snowing and the driving was treacherous. Half way across the road, Fiona heard a car honking. She stopped dead in her tracks, saw two headlights approaching and couldn't move. The next thing she remembered was her father standing over her, as she lay on the road, shouting, "What the hell were you trying to do!"

She had been hit by the oncoming car and thrown forward. Unable to stop, the driver ran over her and she was caught between the front axle and the ground. Fiona was dragged thirty feet as the driver skidded to a stop. She must have said who she was and where she lived, although she had no memory of doing so. On the way to the hospital in the ambulance, the paramedic kept asking Fiona the same questions over and over so she wouldn't fall asleep: What's your name? Where do you live? As the extent of her head injuries were not known, there was a concern that if she fell asleep, she might not wake up. After repeating the questions for the third or fourth time, Fiona replied, "I've already answered those questions. Don't you remember?"

She could hear the siren wailing and wanted to know if they were running any red lights. Once at the hospital she was diagnosed as having suffered a concussion, with a bump the size of a grapefruit on her forehead, two black eyes and a dislocated hip. She spent four weeks in hospital and then five months on crutches.

When it was time for Fiona to return to school following her accident, Ann decided that instead of driving her (why waste gas) she would have Patsy pull Fiona to and from school in their home-made (of course) red, metal wagon. Fiona was mortified and her sister incensed as they bumped and rattled their way down the street to school. Their friends, though, were intrigued and even offered to take turns picking Fiona up and dropping her off in her four-wheeled chariot.

Normally, the girls would come home for lunch but during Fiona's post-accident recuperation they were given permission to remain at school over the noon hour. For the first time, their mother made their lunches for them to take to school. And what an experience that turned out to be! Because Ann Hamilton never threw anything out (twist ties, string, tin foil, plastic containers, waxed paper from bricks of shortening, elastics, etc.), Fiona's and Patsy's sandwiches were always wrapped in plastic bags that had previously contained frozen peas or corn, nylon stockings or rubber gloves. The paper bags that carried the sandwiches were always oversized, stained and well creased from multiple uses. The girls were required to bring home the plastic and paper bags each day – neatly folded. Non compliance with this rule resulted in their mother's use of a plastic sandwich bag bearing a more embarrassing moniker such as toilet paper or a feminine hygiene product.

Hauling Fiona to and from school wasn't the only use the girls made of the wagon (or hurly, as James called it). They were pressed regularly into service by their father to retrieve items he would see on garbage day as he rode his bicycle to the bus stop on his way to work. He would park his bike at a house next to the bus stop and then take the bus the rest of the way. Once at the office, he would call home to give Fiona a description of the items (hoses, carpets, basement windows, TVs, radios or electric motors) and the respective addresses of where they could be found. She had to write them all down and then repeat them to make sure they were correct. It was then up to the sisters to roam the streets, pick up the items and scratch them off the list. Reduce, reuse and recycle were household words at the Hamilton's well before they became part of everyday vocabulary.

The two girls shared a bedroom until Fiona was in Grade 8 at which time they decided they each wanted their own space. They flipped a coin to see who would stay upstairs and who would move into the basement. Fiona won the coin toss and picked the basement, even though no bedroom existed there – yet. Their father had the idea that he wanted to find an old barn in the country, tear it down and rebuild it in their basement as Fiona's bedroom.

For many months the family took trips up the Ottawa Valley to track down dilapidated barns, sheds and outbuildings in farmers' fields. Finally, James settled on a grey one that didn't need much tearing down as most of it had already fallen down. Then they began the process of harvesting the best boards, stacking them and then loading them onto a borrowed flatbed truck. For Fiona and Patsy, it was hard, hot and smelly work. Fiona hoped it would all be worth it, although she couldn't picture herself living in a barn for a bedroom.

Once the boards were unloaded and carried around to the back of the house, Fiona and her father proceeded to pull out as many 'square-headed' nails as they could see. They carted the boards, still covered with dirt and farm animal excrement, down to the basement. The next task involved wire brushes and a yellowish powder that was sprinkled liberally on the boards.

Just as Fiona began to scrub the powder into the first board with her wire brush, James called upstairs, "Ann, if you don't hear from us in the next hour, come and check to see that we're alright."

It wasn't until many years later that Fiona realized the powder they were using so freely with no masks, no gloves and no ventilation was the harmful, carcinogenic chemical DDT.

In the years since Patsy's departure, Fiona had succeeded in suppressing the more unpleasant memories of her sister, but now found it difficult to keep them at bay. Her final year living with Patsy had been particularly difficult. Their worlds couldn't have been further apart. Fiona was a straight-A student in Grade 11 of the 'gifted' program; Patsy, in Grade 9, had been expelled twice, once for fighting and once for swearing at Mrs. Blackthorn, her homeroom teacher. Luckily for Fiona, she and Patsy attended different high schools – the gifted program was not offered at their neighbourhood high school. In that way, Fiona didn't have to suffer the humiliation and possible contamination that would have tainted her high school life because of her sister's erratic behaviour.

Fiona remembered well her mother's account of the last parent/teacher conference she attended on Patsy's behalf that last year. Well-dressed, well-groomed and well-spoken, her mother waited in the hall outside Patsy's homeroom class.

When Mrs. Blackthorn stood in the doorway and called, "Mrs. Hamilton, please," her mother approached the teacher and started to introduce herself.

"I'm sorry," said Mrs. Blackthorn before Ann could say who she was, "but Mrs. Hamilton is next on the list. You'll have to wait your turn, Mrs..."

"But I am Mrs. Hamilton, Patsy Hamilton's mother."

Wide-eyed, Mrs. Blackthorn looked Ann up and down, "Please forgive me, Mrs. Hamilton. Come right in." They both entered the classroom and Mrs. Blackthorn closed the door behind them.

"You are not quite what I had expected," said Mrs. Blackthorn taking her seat and indicating that Ann do the same.

"In what way?"

"Well, to put it delicately, I expected someone much less, shall we say, elegant."

"Whatever do you mean?"

"It's just that your daughter's choice of apparel, personal appearance and general demeanour in no way match your own."

"Could you be more specific?"

Mrs. Blackthorn nodded. "Yesterday, for example, her wardrobe consisted of long, frayed jeans, a threadbare T-shirt and running shoes with no laces. Her hair was dishevelled and hung over her eyes and she fell asleep with her head on the desk."

Mrs. Blackthorn went on to say that Patsy was extremely disruptive in class and used the foulest of language when she was asked to be quiet and sit properly. It was then that Ann made it very clear that Patsy always left home wearing clean, appropriate teenage clothing and that her hair, although somewhat unruly, was always combed and off her face. The picture of this other Patsy that Mrs. Blackthorn was painting in no way resembled her daughter.

When Ann described her encounter with Mrs. Blackthorn later that evening, Fiona knew instantly what was happening. Although Patsy hotly denied everything and shouted that everyone was out to get her, Fiona surmised that her sister was probably popping a pill or two just before heading off to school. She'd then adopt her 'street-kid' look at school and let the drugs cloud her mind and ease her inhibitions. By the end of the day, her buzz would have worn off enough to make herself appear normal at home. But Fiona still said nothing to her parents; she couldn't and wouldn't betray her sister.

It was shortly after that parent/teacher conference that Patsy ended up in hospital with hepatitis from using a dirty syringe. And to think that Patsy was just sixteen – the same age as Jesse – when Fiona saw her for the last time. The thought made her shudder.

Chapter 23

Cold, wet November gave way to cold, snowy December. Jesse underwent his last chemotherapy and radiation treatment. Robbed of his strength, his immune system and his hair, he looked frail and vulnerable as Fiona sat with him to wait for the doctor to tell them whether he was strong enough to proceed with the bone marrow transplant.

"I'll be really bummed if Doctor Huard says I'm not ready," said Jesse with a weak smile.

"We have to be prepared for that," said Fiona, "but all the news we've had so far has been good." And with that the doctor entered the room with what Fiona guessed was a smile beneath his mask.

"Jesse," said Dr. Huard, "some days I don't like being a doctor because I have to tell patients things they may not want to hear. Today is not one of those days!"

"You mean we can go ahead with the transplant?" asked Jesse.

"The sooner, the better," replied Dr. Huard, as he patted Jesse's shoulder. "Mrs. Hamilton, we've booked your procedure for first thing tomorrow morning. Does that suit you?"

"I'll have to check my agenda," Fiona teased, "but I'm sure I can rearrange my schedule."

Fiona rushed home to tell everyone the good news. She was both excited and nervous at the same time; excited that she would be giving Jesse a fighting chance at a full recovery and nervous that it would fail. Michael made dinner, Connor did all the dishes and Fiona was ordered to either sit and put her feet up or relax in the hot tub and then sit and put her feet up. She chose the latter, along with a steaming cup of her favourite tea.

Fiona, accompanied by Michael and Connor, arrived at the hospital early the following morning. They both hugged her, said how proud they were of her and then waved goodbye as she headed down the hall toward the day surgery unit.

The nurse who greeted her explained what the procedure would entail and then handed Fiona a hospital gown and showed her where to change and leave her clothes. Once into the gown, she was escorted to the operating room where she was asked to lie down on the operating table. Dr. Huard appeared moments later and assured her that everything would be fine; that she would feel only slight discomfort during the procedure and that it would be over before she knew it.

True to his word, Dr. Huard worked quickly and efficiently to harvest enough of Fiona's bone marrow for the transfusion. In the recovery room, Fiona had a chance to think about all the positive stories she would tell Jesse about his mother. She knew his recovery would take much longer and be much more arduous than hers. She would have to come up with the different ways in which she could keep him motivated, keep his spirits up and encourage him with the power of positive thinking.

By late afternoon, Fiona was dressed and waiting for Michael to pick her up and take her home. As she saw him approach the waiting room, she wondered whether he had any news about Jesse.

"Hey, you don't look half bad," said Michael smiling as he leaned down to give her a kiss. "I'm so proud of you, my love."

"Don't get too close," said Fiona, "I must smell like I've been dunked in a vat of antiseptic. My hip is a little sore, but other than that I feel fine."

"Come on, let's get you home. Connor is making dinner – candles, the good silverware and all."

"I hope he isn't going to too much trouble. I don't have much of an appetite. Have you any news about Jesse?"

"He's making tomato soup and toast soldiers just like you used to make the kids when they weren't feeling well. And yes, I have news about Jesse," said Michael as he led Fiona out of the hospital to the car.

On their way home, Michael recounted Dr. Huard's explanation of how Fiona's bone marrow was infused through Jesse's vein in his arm, similar to a blood transfusion. Prior to the infusion, special filters had been used to remove bone fragments and fatty particles. Jesse was resting comfortably and would be able to receive visitors in the morning, provided he was not suffering any adverse reactions.

Connor was waiting in the driveway and helped his mother out of the car. "Are you feeling alright, Mum?" he asked.

"Just a little stiff. I hear you've made dinner."

"I got a few tips from Lindsay and Frances but the menu is all mine!" said Connor as they entered the kitchen.

Fiona could see the dining room table had been set with her grandmother's sterling silver cutlery, Royal Dolton china and Stewart crystal glassware. The room glowed from the light of a myriad of candles, as Connor pulled out his mother's chair at the head of the table. Fiona squeezed his hand as she sat down and motioned for him to bring her some tissues. "Yes, the waterworks have started again," she said, laughing and crying at the same time.

After they had been served their soup and toast soldiers, Connor lifted his glass of milk to toast his mother. "It's not every day you can thank somebody for saving someone's life. Thanks, Mum for saving Jesse's. I love you very much."

"Here, here," said Michael, "I second that toast."

Over coffee they talked about Jesse and how he would need their love and support once he was released from hospital. It would take months for him to regain his strength. Up to now, no one had mentioned or questioned where Jesse would go to convalesce. Finally, Connor broached the subject by suggesting that since Jesse's original decision to stay with them was based on their close proximity to the Children's Hospital, then maybe he could be convinced to make his stay with them permanent. He also offered to act as Jesse's chauffeur, once he passed his driver's licence, to take him for check-ups or tests or doctor's appointments – even if it meant missing classes.

Fiona nodded in agreement and then asked Connor what stories she should tell Jesse to keep his spirits up and to help him get to know his mother and their family better.

"There are so many funny ones," said Connor, "but my favourite is the one about how Grandad used to wake you and Patsy up every morning."

Fiona laughed out loud as she remembered her father coming into their bedroom each morning, as if appearing on stage, opening his arms wide, drawing back the curtains with dramatic flourish and saying,

"Awake! For morning in the bowl of night,

Hath cast the stone that put the stars to flight:

And lo! The hunter of the East hath caught

The Sultan's turret in a noose of light."

She and her sister would groan, hide under their covers and beg him to leave. When Fiona was younger, she thought her father was saying 'hath caught the Sultan's turd in a noose of light', which sent her into fits of laughter.

There were others, too, like:

"Night's candles are burnt out, and jocund day

Stands tiptoe on the misty mountain tops."

None of her friends had fathers who would recite The Rubayyat of Omar Khayyam or Shakespeare's Romeo and Juliet on a daily basis. At the time, she thought it was the strangest thing; but now she marvelled at how she could remember every word and picture every gesture.

Chapter 24

The phone rang the next morning as Fiona was sitting in bed with her breakfast tray that groaned under the weight of coffee, cereal, toast with ginger jam (her favourite) and raspberry yogurt. It stopped ringing just as she reached over to answer. Connor appeared at the bedroom doorway, "It's Gran calling to see how you are. I told her you were 'resting comfortably' and she laughed out loud." He handed her the phone.

"That's just how Grandad would say it!" said Fiona as she took the handset and gave him a thank-you kiss. "Hi Mum. I had an uneventful night and Connor is right, I am resting comfortably."

"That's a relief," said her mother. "Is there anything I can do for you today? I could make macaroni and cheese for your dinner tonight."

"Sure, Mum that would be great. I might need you to go to the drug store. I'm running low on Advil. Dr. Huard has given me some heavy-duty pain medication but I'd like to see if I can manage with the over-the-counter variety."

"Of course, I can. I'll stop by on my way back from delivering Meals-on Wheels. Should I send your father over for lunch?"

"As long as he brings some for me too; some of his tried-and-true vegetable soup with toast and stilton cheese would suit me just fine."

Fiona could tell by the tremor in her mother's voice that she wanted to say much more but was unable to steer the conversation away from housekeeping issues, pleasantries and offers of help. Fiona had never heard the words 'I love you' from either of her parents; not that it bothered her. She understood the era in which they grew up where children were truly seen and not heard.

In her mother's case she was both unseen and unheard in the literal not the figurative sense. Fiona's well-to-do grandparents had sent Ann away to boarding school on the train by herself from Ottawa to Montreal at the tender age of ten. Her eight-year experience at Trafalgar School for Young Girls scarred her for life. Alone and unloved, she hated it and wasn't encouraged to come home until she had graduated from McGill University and then Royal Victoria Nursing School at the age of 28. Ann Hamilton never forgave her parents for effectively abandoning her and denying her a nurturing, caring home life. And she vowed never to send her children to boarding school. Fiona and Tim were the only cousins on their mother's side who had attended public school – much to Ann's siblings' horror.

Fiona's father, on the other hand, grew up in his bachelor uncle's grand house in the north of Scotland, where James had gone to live with his mother and brother after their father had died. His mother, for all intents and purposes, took on the role of housekeeper and hostess for her brother. Seeing his mother in a subservient role and watching his uncle lead a frivolous and self-indulgent life did little to prepare James for fatherhood.

Fiona knew her parents loved her and were proud of her, even though they couldn't bring themselves to say the words. She knew, too, that they would back her in whatever venture she embarked on or decision she took. When she and Michael founded their firm, Hamilton and Kellaher, her parents were their silent partners; with funds at the ready should they be needed. So when Ann Hamilton offered to make dinner or to pick up something from the drug store or to send her father over with lunch, it was her way of telling Fiona how much she loved her.

The next time the phone rang that morning, it was Dr. Huard inquiring about Fiona's state of recovery and to tell her that Jesse had spiked a fever during the night but that he had not shown any other signs of rejection – particularly hives or shortness of breath. He also told her that Jesse could start receiving visitors later in the afternoon.

Fiona let out a sigh of relief and thanked Dr. Huard profusely for his help. He returned the compliment and told her the next few weeks might be like riding a roller-coaster. He advised her to get lots of rest and to not get discouraged should Jesse take a turn for the worse. In his experience, the support and encouragement from a loving family was just as effective as medication in helping patients through the healing process.

Her next call was to Michael to let him know the good news. He told Fiona he would pick Connor up from school and then they could all go to see Jesse.

Fiona made sure to be ready and waiting when Michael arrived to take them to the hospital. It had taken her a good deal longer than usual to get dressed and put her face on; but she was determined to show Jesse that she wasn't suffering from her procedure.

Upon arriving at the isolation ward, Fiona, Michael and Connor were asked to gown up from head to toe. They then proceeded cautiously into Jesse's room where they found him sitting up listening to his Walkman. As soon as he saw them, his face lit up and he reached out both arms. Of course, Fiona was the first to take advantage of the open invitation for a hug – gingerly though it was.

Speaking through her mask and her tears, Fiona said, "I hope when your hair grows back, it's red like mine!"

"Two red-heads in the family," said Michael, patting Jesse's shoulder warmly, "I don't know if we can survive that."

"Hey Jesse," said Connor, as he handed him the latest issue of *Car and Driver.* "Do you think they'll let you out for Christmas?"

"All they say is 'We have to take it one day at a time'," said Jesse. "But so far, things have gone pretty smoothly. How are you feeling, Fiona?"

"I'm a little slower than usual but all in all, I feel fine," replied Fiona.

They talked about what Jesse could expect in terms of his recovery; milestones like regaining his appetite, his strength and his hair and then left him to get a good night's sleep.

Over the next several weeks, Fiona visited Jesse daily, sometimes supplementing his diet with cheeseburgers and milkshakes and always feeding his insatiable curiosity about his mother. She told him about how one of their favourite after-dinner activities, when they lived on the prairie, was to drive down with their father to the Suffield train station, arriving precisely at ten minutes to seven. They would then take pennies – only two each – and put them on the track, stand back and wait for the seven o'clock arrival of the 'The Canadian' that would roar past the station, flattening their pennies into the size of silver dollars. Their father made sure to hold their hands tightly, to prevent them from being sucked into the train's wake.

The girls would squeal with delight and wave at the blur of passengers who were seated behind the windows. The whole episode lasted less than ten seconds. It took much longer for them to find their pennies – still hot to the touch – and take them home.

James Hamilton had a life-long fascinating with trains, particularly steam trains and with Christmas fast approaching, Fiona knew it would soon be time to help bring up the 'Ralston Railroad' from her parents' basement and set it up on the front porch. No plain, ordinary Christmas lights, Santa or reindeer for the Hamilton house; instead James had built a one-dimensional steam engine to scale out of plywood, painted black and gold. It came complete with piston-turning wheels, a clanging bell, a brilliant headlamp and belching smoke stack. There was also a conductor swinging a train lantern, a red-and-black passenger car named 'The Chinook' and a flashing railway crossing signal. Lugging it in and out of the basement each Christmas was no small feat. But it was worth all the effort to see the delight in the faces of people, young and old, who came from miles around to watch and hear the symphony of train sounds that was music to James' ears.

Decorating the Christmas tree was also slightly out of the ordinary at the Hamilton's when the children were young. The tree itself always had to be chopped, whittled and shimmed to fit into a special holder that James had made. It consisted of a long, metal pipe that was attached to a round wooden disc. There was no give to the pipe so the tree trunk had to be made to fit – somehow. After much shouting and arguing, the tree always appeared crooked and had to be spun around in order to hide the inevitable imperfections and missing branches.

The lights, baubles and tinsel all had to be placed on the tree in a certain order. Each strand of tinsel was unwound from the cardboard holder (where it had been carefully stored after having been painstakingly retrieved from last year's tree and the one before and the one before that) and placed individually on separate branches. Fiona never remembered seeing or opening a new package of tinsel. She remembered one year when Patsy thought it would be fun to just throw handfuls of the stuff at the tree to see where it would land. Their mother did not find it amusing and made them pick it all off and start again.

Christmas morning was a strict and regimented affair. Fiona, Patsy and Tim were permitted to open their stockings and one present – from an immediate family member – before their parents got up. Once James and Ann joined them, everyone was given a sheet of paper and pen to record their gifts and a knife to carefully cut the tape from the wrapping so that the paper could be folded neatly and reused next Christmas. The centre rolls from toilet paper were used to wind ribbon so that it too could be recycled. Each one took his or her turn to open gifts, making sure to read aloud the card from the gift-giver. Once the gift was opened, it was passed around, appraised and duly recorded so that a thank-you note could be written.

Having witnessed his wife's delight in the Hamilton Christmas train and her inherited love of trains in general, Michael had taken Fiona for her 40th birthday on the famous Orient Express. They travelled from London to Paris to Venice to Istanbul in the distinctive shiny blue and gold cars topped with bright white roofs. Inside, the highly polished and lacquered walls inlaid with mahogany made Fiona feel like they were on the movie set from Agatha Christie's *Murder on the Orient Express* and she loved every minute of it. They were surrounded by luxury and elegance of every description – velvet, silver, etched glass and silk brocade. The fully-restored cars were designed and built from the early 1900s to the 1930s – each one now bearing a brass plaque highlighting its history. Some cars had fallen into disrepair during the 40s and 50s, while others had been used as hotels, hospitals and even brothels.

Following their once-in-a-lifetime trip, Fiona and Michael were in the middle of showing her parents their photographs when her father suddenly left the kitchen table and headed down to the basement. Several minutes later he returned and handed Fiona two oblong packages, the size of French baguettes, wrapped in newspaper and tied with string. Puzzled, Fiona took the packages and opened them. To her surprise, one was a steam engine from a model train; the other a passenger car that looked identical to the Orient Express car in their photographs. In fact, the serial number on the model car was only 10 digits off the actual car that Fiona and Michael had ridden in.

"What's this, Dad?" asked Fiona.

"It was called the 'Blue Train' when I was a child. I asked my mother for it at Christmas when I was 8 years old. It was my pride and joy. Eventually, I collected ten cars, including the dining car, the bar car and the coal tender. I ran the track the full length of the car shed our house – Blackfriars. My Uncle JR was none too pleased when there was no longer room to park his Jaguar! I'd like you to have it as a memento of your historic trip."

Fiona gingerly inspected the engine and the passenger car and then hugged her father tightly. The engine, the coal tender and one 'wagon-lit' were now mounted on two pieces of track and proudly displayed on the window ledge in Fiona's kitchen.

Chapter 25

In the weeks following Jesse's and Fiona's surgery, Connor's life regained its normal routine. Christmas exams were upon him and this year he was determined to put more effort into his studies. Of course, it helped that Lindsay had offered to be his 'study buddy'. And, he certainly didn't want to look like a slacker in her eyes.

Worcester Academy was still riding high after its highly successful and well-publicized blood donor drive and Connor could hear his name being whispered as he travelled the corridors to and from class. It surprised him to admit that he even missed Frances at home and sought her out regularly at school to give her updates about his mother and Jesse. She told him she'd had enough of being her mother's nursemaid was looking forward to coming home for Christmas.

"Do you think the doctors will let Jesse come home for Christmas?" asked Frances.

"I think my Mum asks every day. But all they say is 'we're taking it one day at a time', whatever that means."

"Well, there's only a few weeks left and Jesse hasn't had any major set-backs."

"I went to see him yesterday and for the first time I didn't have to wear a mask and a gown. He told me that by the end of the week he should be out of the isolation ward."

"That's great news. Hey, you haven't given me your Christmas list yet. Don't tell me you've be too busy with Lindsay to write one."

"Very funny. For your information, I have it in my locker. And where is yours, I might ask?"

"I'm just putting the final touches on it. I'll give it to you tomorrow," said Frances.

The two of them then discussed what type of gift they should get for their parents. They usually gave Fiona and Michael a combined gift like a certificate to their favourite restaurant or a basket filled with their favourite coffee, chocolates, cookies and jams. This year it was Connor's turn to pool their money, shop for the gift and then Frances would wrap it.

"Should we get something for Jesse, too?" asked Connor.

"For sure. What do you think he'd like? We don't have much to spend."

"Well, my Mum has been telling him all kinds of crazy stories about her life with Patsy. Some of them are pretty funny. Maybe we could get her to write them down and then we could turn them into a book or something and give it to Jesse."

"That's a great idea. And you could illustrate them."

"Mum has found tons of photos in Gran's basement. I could put some of those in too. I'll call you tonight and we can make a list of the things we want to include in the Christmas basket for my Mum and your Dad."

Connor then made his way to the library to meet Lindsay. Ever since he'd planned the donor drive he found himself gravitating to the library to study, conduct research and even get started on his class assignments. Maybe there was something to this studying thing – good marks, high praise from parents and endless encouragement from a certain southern belle.

Lindsay waved to him as he rounded the corner past the registration desk.

"Hey Lindsay," whispered Connor as he reached her table.

"Hey Connor," Lindsay whispered back clearing a space for Connor to set down his books and papers. "What's the latest news about Jesse?"

"He seems to be getting stronger every day. We even think he might be able to come home for Christmas Day."

"That would be fantastic! Be sure to tell him I'll come and visit when I get back from Georgia."

"Mr. Munro and Miss Giffen," called Mrs. Beachy, in her reedy, high-pitched voice, "the library is not a venue for conducting private conversations. Should you wish to continue, please have the common courtesy to do so outside."

With that, Connor and Lindsay packed up their schoolwork and made their way to the drop-off circle, where Lindsay's embassy limo was waiting patiently. Just as they approached the car, Lindsay stopped, took Jesse's hand and pulled him behind one of the two stone pillars that flanked the entrance. The next thing he knew, Lindsay was giving him a warm hug and kissing him lightly on the lips. It was over in a matter of moments but it made Connor feel as if time were standing still.

"I've been wanting to do that for the longest time," sighed Lindsay. "I hope I wasn't too forward. My mother always says I act first and think second. Are you OK, Connor? You look a little freaked out."

"Umm ... yeah. I'm just fine, Lindsay," replied Connor slightly dazed but smiling. "I'm glad you made the first move. I couldn't work up enough courage!"

"See you after the holidays," laughed Lindsay as she waved and headed toward the limo.

That evening at dinner, Connor related his and Frances' idea of creating a memory book for Jesse. Fiona and Michael loved it and Fiona said she would be delighted to write down the stories she'd already told Jesse and would think of a few more to add as well. Michael offered to have it printed and bound.

Sitting with her cup of coffee after dinner, Fiona thought about other stories and reminiscences that could be included in Jesse's memory book. She wanted him to get a better understanding of his mother's early life and to show him that she truly was one of the family.

Of course, she had to describe to Jesse what it was like for Fiona, Patsy and Tim to be pronounced sick enough by their mother to stay home from school. According to Ann, just because you were running a high fever or throwing up or coughing – enough to keep you home from school – didn't mean you should be idle. Confined to bed with no TV and no telephone – yes; but idle – no, never. Cleaning out the kitchen junk drawer, organizing plastic containers (trying to match them with the corresponding lids) or sorting through the mitten basket, while lying in bed, were regular assignments. Fiona smiled as she realized that she, too, often asked Connor and Frances to 'help around the house' when they were feeling under the weather.

Equipped with a bell that was to be rung to alert their mother to only the most urgent of needs, Fiona and her siblings were kept occupied during their confinement by listening to albums from Broadway musicals and Gilbert and Sullivan comic operas that their mother stacked on the record player. Fiona, Patsy and Tim knew all the words to the songs from *The Pajama Game*, *South Pacific*, *The Mikado*, *The Pirates of Penzance*, *Oklahoma* and *Annie Get Your Gun*.

In fact, Fiona knew the words to one particular song from Rogers and Hammerstein's *South Pacific* a little too well. When she was in grade two, each student was asked to come to the front of the class and sing their favourite song. After many off-key renditions of *Mary Had a Little Lamb*, *Twinkle, Twinkle Little Star* and *Frère Jacques* sung by the other boys and girls, Fiona stood confidently in front of all her classmates and belted out the song entitled *Bloody Mary*. The words for this particular song are as follows:

Bloody Mary is the girl I love,

Bloody Mary is the girl I love,

Bloody Mary is the girl I love.

Now, ain't that too damn bad!

Her teacher, Mrs. Duncansen, didn't know whether to laugh, clap or scold. She ended up smiling, nodding and making a mental note to telephone Ann Hamilton after school. Fiona curtseyed and returned to her seat, wondering why her classmates had such puzzled looks on their faces. Fiona would be sure to sing the song to Jesse, just to see the look on his face!

She would also describe to Jesse his mother's delight in attending Ralston's annual village bazaar held at the Recreation Centre. The sisters would eagerly start their day at the one-and-only coffee shop where Patsy would order a chocolate milkshake and a grilled cheese. Fiona always had a root beer float and an order of cinnamon toast. They would then make their way to the bazaar where there would be a maze of tables and booths selling books, jewellery, hand-knitted items, used kitchen appliances, tools and toys. Their favourite booth was 'The Fish Pond' where, for five cents each, the girls would fish for a prize using a broom handle with a string tied to the end. They would cast their lines over a cardboard wall that had been painted with an 'underwater' scene. Giggling as they waited anxiously for the tug on the strings, they would reel in their prizes – usually a comb, a mirror, a pencil or a yoyo. They were never disappointed with their 'catch of the day'.

At one year's bazaar, Fiona spied a particularly fetching hat displayed prominently on one of the tables festooned with brightly coloured ladies' gloves and scarves. This one-of-a-kind bonnet was made with blue silk and had lovely brown lace ties that wrapped around the brim. Fiona tried it on, tied the lace ribbons into a big bow under her chin, looked in the mirror and thought the hat suited her quite well. Patsy readily agreed. Fiona bought it for fifty cents – a fortune to her– and proudly wore it to Sunday school the next day. She expected to receive compliments; what she didn't expect was to have her brother pointing his finger and laughing at her, telling everyone that she was actually wearing a lampshade! Crushed, and heartbroken, she cried all the way home.

Later that evening, Patsy offered Fiona her favourite marble – a navy blue one with gold swirls – hoping to make her sister feel better. It did. Much to her surprise, Fiona still had that marble. She would take it with her on her next visit to see Jesse and give it to him once she had explained its significance. She hoped it would bring him a sense of comfort to know that his mother, at such a young age, had given away one of her most prized possessions, in order to console her sister.

Chapter 26

Jesse was making steady progress. He'd had a few setbacks; a chest infection and slight numbness in his fingers. With a week to go before Christmas, Fiona met with Dr. Huard to discuss the possibility of Jesse being able to spend time at home over the holidays. She hoped he could stay with them for at least Christmas Eve and Christmas Day but she would settle for a couple of hours.

Fiona sat nervously in the waiting room of Dr. Huard's office. His nurse called her in.

"Good morning Mrs. Hamilton," said Dr. Huard. "I have excellent news for you." He had Jesse's medical file open on the desk in front of him.

"I'm glad to hear it," replied Fiona as she took a seat. "We're hoping you will let Jesse spend Christmas at home with us."

"That's exactly what I'd like him to do. He needs to have a change of scenery and his prognosis is excellent. I've never seen such a rapid recovery. There are always medical reasons for a patient's improvement but I firmly believe that there are also non-medical reasons. In Jesse's case, I feel he wants to get better to be with you and your family. I sense he has heightened energy after you and Connor have visited with him."

"It's funny you should say that, Dr. Huard, because we make a conscious effort to send 'positive vibes', as Connor calls them, to Jesse."

"Well, they must be working because I think he should be able to go home on Christmas Eve and stay with you until the New Year," said Dr. Huard as he stood, leaned over his desk and shook Fiona's hand.

"Thank you Dr. Huard," said Fiona smiling. "This is the best Christmas present we could have asked for."

Fiona left Dr. Huard's office and headed straight for Jesse's room. She knew Connor was visiting him and she couldn't wait to tell them both the good news. As she entered his room, they were engrossed in their Game Boys and hardly noticed her.

"Excuse me gentlemen, but would either of you be interested to know that we will have an extra special visitor for Christmas?" asked Fiona.

Both boys looked at her expectantly, as Fiona slowly nodded her head and smiled. As it dawned on them what she meant, they said in unison, "For real?"

"I've just met with Dr. Huard and he has given us the green light. Jesse can come home on Christmas Eve and stay right through until the New Year," said Fiona.

"That's the best news, Mum", said Connor.

"It's what I was wishing for," said Jesse, "but I didn't want to get my hopes up. Just think, this time next week I'll be able to wake up without the smell of disinfectant and the constant prodding and poking by the nurses and doctors."

The rest of the week progressed at a snail's pace until, at last, it was time for Fiona and Connor to pick up Jesse from the hospital. Michael and Frances were putting the final touches on the Memory Book they had made for Jesse and Ann was busy in Fiona's kitchen putting the final touches on her Christmas shortbread cookies – trying, without success, to keep her husband from testing too many before she had them perfectly arranged on the plate. Frances and Connor had made a large 'Welcome HOME Jesse' sign that Michael had stuck in the snow bank at the end of the driveway so that it would be the first thing Jesse saw as he approached the house.

Connor called from the car to tell everyone to get ready. As they rounded the corner, Jesse saw the sign; he saw Michael; he saw Ann and James Hamilton; and for the first time he saw Frances.

"Connor," said Jesse, "I thought you told me Frances was your stepsister."

"She is," replied Connor.

"Man, she looks just like you. She could even be your twin!"

But that's another story.

Questions for Discussion

1. In what ways is Fiona like her mother? How does she differ?

2. There is very little description of what the characters look like. How did this affect you as you read the book?

3. Why did Ann treat Fiona and Patsy like twins?

4. Why did Fiona never try to find her sister?

5. Why was Connor so affected by Jesse's plight?

6. Describe the similarities and differences in Connor's and Jesse's lives.

7. Fiona and Patsy were treated equally as young girls; why did they grow into such different women?

8. Ann and James Hamilton disowned Patsy because of her behavior; what would you have done?

9. Should Patsy have reconnected with her family for Jesse's sake?

10. How would Jesse's life have been different had he known his family?

11. Why did Connor not confront Jesse about stealing his Walkman?

12. Why did Connor's insistence on getting a new Walkman fade?

13. How did you feel about Ann's reaction to Jesse?

14. Did you find that James' feelings toward Jesse were true?

15. Why did Fiona not think twice about helping Jesse?

16. Did Fiona take a chance by inviting Jesse into her home?

17. What happens next?

CPSIA information can be obtained at www.ICGtesting.com
Printed in the USA
LVOW081727011111

253045LV00010B/21/P

9 781426 967368